# SURRENDERED VII

# BY

## Peggy Patrick

ISBN-13:  978-0-9962959-6-3

Cover Design by Charlene Raddon
http://cover-ops.blogspot.com

# SURRENDERED VII

# CHAPTER ONE

The weight on her chest got heavier each time she tried to push against it. There was no pain in her body, anywhere, but the pressure was causing great emotional pain—of pure fear. But she *had* to fight. With all the breath and strength she could summon, she pushed hard. An exploding cry spit inside her head like shattered glass.

She forced her eyes open, a small audible cry escaping from deep down as she struggled to breathe normally.

"Oh, God! Oh, God!"

She had tried so hard not to fall asleep. Every night was the same fight to remain awake until she had no more say in the matter. She *had* to sleep—but, why did she have to endure these relentless nightmares every night? *Something* was always trying to crush the life out of her or chase her down until her legs would give out and she collapsed. The *thing* always got her and tormented her until she finally returned to consciousness and thankfully awakened.

Belle Anne sat up, sucked in a couple of deep breaths and scrambled her medium length, dirty-blonde hair with her fingers until her big loose curls fell into their usual place. Her easy hair-do was her only claim to perfection—finger it and go.

In fact, her hair was the only thing she liked about herself. Her clothes were always wrong no matter what she wore. She either looked too frumpy or old enough to be her own grandmother. Why she bothered with makeup, she couldn't say. But going out of the house without a full face of foundation and *some* mascara on her eyes was unthinkable—as much so as heading out without her underwear on.

But—today was the day! She had waited for this most of her life but had counted down the days for the past two months for it to actually be real. Her eye spotted the worn taupe cowboy boots and extra-long pre-washed wrangler jeans she had laid on the floor beside her bed a week ago. A fresh wave of excitement forced the lingering effects of the nightmare aside as she bounded into her luxurious split-level bathroom to start getting ready.

For two glorious weeks, Belle Anne James was going to experience her dream vacation. She was headed to Jackson Hole, Wyoming to High Point Dude Ranch after reserving one full week in a log cabin and the second week in an authentic Indian teepee—horseback riding, chuckwagon food. The pictures on their website had stirred her excitement into a ridiculous giddiness.

All her life, as far back as she could recall, she'd been drawn to the old west movies on TV, local rodeos in her North Texas and Southern Oklahoma neighborhood. Watching the cowboys and cowgirls loping around an arena or occasionally clip-clopping down the street in front of her house where she lived with her parents, made her want to chase after them and beg for a ride.

But that was all part of her secret life—her hopes and dreams. Not in a million years would she so much as allude to those desires to a living soul. There was no one to trust.

Belle Anne learned early on to hold anything that meant something to her in a special place inside her heart where it couldn't be found—Or else, that too would be ripped away from her and destroyed.

It was next to impossible to stop the onslaught of words and pictures that slammed through her mind once they got started. And even the promise of a dream coming to pass—like today—didn't stop that from happening. Before she realized it, her mind drifted backward into that dark place she hated with her whole soul.

It always seemed to begin with the same mental image of her walking into the restroom of her Junior High school when she was eleven years old and a sixth grader. Tears were wetting her cheeks and she walked to the sink to wet a paper towel she'd pulled from the holder on the wall. But when she looked into the mirror, she gasped. Her face wasn't just wet. It was smeared with blood. She glanced down. Her white blouse was streaked with red runs all over the front. She froze, not knowing what to do for herself. There was no one to call—No way to get more clothes.

Suddenly the door opened behind her and a glance in the mirror told her one of the teachers who was in the office when she stepped in to sign in late and get a pass to her first period class, had followed her. The lady didn't say a word but got another paper towel and dabbed at the bloody mess on her face. Then just as silently, walked back out. There was nothing to do but go to class.

Then the image changed. Her mother had a wad of her shoulder length auburn hair in her fist and slung her across the wide central hallway of their home until she saw, rather than felt, herself slam against the wall, face first. Her school books that she had so carefully stacked and held in the crook of her arm went flying all over the hallway along with homework papers that flew out of her loose-leaf notebook. While she tried to gather up the mess, her mother kicked her in her private parts—front and back—and screamed vile, filthy curses and names at her—"clean it up…clean it up"—all the time, kicking her again and again. "Walk to school! You're stupid and ugly!"

Belle Anne came back to reality and stood frozen in front of her own sink and mirror. She stared at the young blonde woman with wide, hazel eyes that were drowning in pain. Her face was one thing her mother had right—She *was* ugly—until she covered it with her eyes and face full of makeup and a box of blonde shampoo-in color to cover the dull red hair. Not great—but at least she could pretend she was a *sort of pretty* someone else.

She consoled herself with the knowledge that no one on this vacation would know the real Belle Anne—not even her name. Belle Anne. She hated the sound of that name, no matter who was saying it. It had been used like a curse word all of her life and no matter who spoke the name now, her cringe was automatic.

For the next two weeks, she would only hear a nickname she chose for herself. *Daisy.* Daisy James. She loved daisies. The name had a soft, free, unfettered sound—something you would find out in the open fields, living off of sunshine and warm breezes.

With her excitement refreshed, she finished dressing in extra-long Wrangler jeans, boots and a white V-neck short-sleeved T-shirt. She twirled around in front of the floor length mirror and smiled.

*Double OO Ranch, Jackson Hole, Wyoming*
The sun was hot and as usual, the wind was blowing. It was a warm wind, but much appreciated by the cowboys, horses and dogs alike. None dared to complain about the blowing dust.

Clint Berry and Mitch Corry were the newest hands at High Point Dude Ranch. They were the lone occupants of the four-man bunk house located on the far backside of the ranch. Both were well-seasoned cowboys who hired out from time to time to the Double OO Cattle Ranch about five miles down the road from High Point—like today.

Mitch twisted his sooty navy-blue neckerchief around and pulled it up to cover his mouth and nose. Clint saw the swirl of dust racing toward them at the same time and followed suit.

"Close your eyes, Tuff," Mitch warned his gelding and oldest friend of fifteen years. Both men turned their horses' rear ends to the blowing silt and sat still until it passed.

On their way again, they uncovered their mouths. Trail dust was one thing, but these sudden whirlwinds of dirt left their clothes and exposed skin, thick brown—eyes gritty. Neither bothered to make any pointless small talk about needing rain.

Judd Luke, owner of the Double OO, as well as Pastor at the ranch's Cowboy Church, had hired them for a couple days of rounding up several mama cow and calf pairs that had strayed off somewhere away from the herd. Their main jobs were on the dude ranch and consisted of various duties such as heading up the trail rides for the guests or pulling a tractor with a long trailer of hay riders for a ranch tour and wiener roast in the red rock canyons. Either way, there was never a dull moment. Days were long and sometimes pressured trying to keep all the *dudes* free from injury and alive. Days could be purely exhausting, dirty and sweaty—or freezing cold—but, the contentment in these wranglers' souls could only be understood by another who lived the cowboy life.

Mitch Corry was born and raised in Wyoming, just a little south of Jackson on his family's thousand-acre cattle ranch. First his mom, and then his dad, had illnesses the past few years that eventually claimed both of their lives and forced the sale of the ranch to pay off the medical debts.

He and his family had attended Cowboy Church at High Point for a couple of years and when the ranch sold, Jesse Brandon came to see him and offered a job. Thankfully, he was allowed to do day-work for the Double OO during slow times at the dude ranch—such as today. This was his real passion—chasing cattle across hundreds of acres, branding season and every aspect of cattle ranching. He'd been doing it for most of his thirty years, except for a four-year stint in the United States Marines. But he *did* surprisingly enjoy the banter with the families that visited from around the country.

"Mitch, head out around that crop of trees there." Clint pointed a leather gloved finger toward the left of the beaten path they were following. "I'll head toward the backside of the creek. It's fairly brushy. Those mama's like to hide em there."

Mitch nodded and reined Tuff due south toward the tall trees off in the distance.

Clint kicked his blue roan ranch gelding into a fast trot through the low sage brush. Riding alone across this wild Wyoming prairie with the glorious Wind River Mountains on the horizon—what more could a man want for a work place. He'd worked in law-enforcement earlier on and done quite a bit of investigative police work, but his heart was here, for more reasons than the cowboy work, such as—Abigail Luke—Abby and her baby boy, who was less than a year old.

He'd watched little David come into the world in the hospital delivery room—a result of the rape of his young mother only a couple weeks after she'd left home for college.

Clint was cowboying for High Point at the time and happened to be the one standing in front of Abby the night she melted down and confessed what had happened to her. He knew Almighty God had placed him there for her that night. He'd left the ranch shortly after to hook up with his friends from a private investigators service in order to find and bring to justice a group of rapists who had lured her, along with other young women, into a trap. With that accomplished, he returned to work for Jesse Brandon at High Point.

By then, Mitch Corry had hired on and moved into the bunk house. He joined him and here he was, living his dream and biding his time until he could take a closer step toward the one woman in all the world that he loved. He felt it was in her best interest to give her a wide berth of space—time to allow her emotions to heal. And little David. He would give him his name along with the rest of the universe the day Abby took his name as well.

He forced his concentration back to the task at hand, as much as possible. He was eager to finish this particular day. Abby and baby David were coming to try out his bunkhouse culinary skills this evening.

Mitch thankfully chose to eat with the ranch gang at Hank's chuckwagon.


Abby smiled in his direction as Mitch and his jangling spurs entered the small living space of the bunkhouse. He was carrying a hand full of calf ropes he'd borrowed from Andy Parker, figuring this was a good time to return them. He had only taken enough time to wash his face, hands and arms, but there wasn't time to shower before Hank would be dishing up supper. Most of the hands came in their dirt and sweat for the same reason, so he felt in good company.

"Hello, Abby. Hey there, cowboy," he greeted the pair as they came through the front door, David perched on his mom's hip.

"Hi, Mitch. Something smells wonderful in here."

He grinned. "Promise you it's not me."

"That's for sure," a voice rolled in from the kitchen. Clint greeted Abby with a kiss on her forehead while David reached chubby little arms out toward him, squealing with joy. He took him and guided Abby toward the kitchen with an arm around her shoulders.

"Hey—I know when I'm not wanted." Mitch headed outside still mumbling. "I don't always stink, ya know. My horse loves me, even if I do."

Muffled laughter trailed him off the porch and he opened the truck door. "Come on, SaraLou," he smooched at Clint's Aussie pup and she happily leaped inside. "I'm taking the dog!" He yelled out the window, then headed for the ranch yard.

He didn't know if Clint heard him or not, but SaraLou went off with Mitch every chance she got, and Clint *did* know that. Mitch tried to make him promise to leave her to him in his will, but all he could get from his bunkmate was an eye-roll.

Mitch reached an arm around his supper date's thick, furry neck and rubbed his hand up and down her shoulder. "We make a good team, huh? You're my girl."

She whined, danced her front legs on the truck seat and licked a few small slobbers on the side of his face. When he pulled up and parked beside the ranch house, she jumped in his lap and scratched feverishly on the window to get out.

"Ok! Ok! Hold your paws." He swung the door open and watched her leap to the ground and race to meet the equally excited *Sunshine Logan.* The shepard/golden retriever mix had been adopted by Andy and Summer Parker a few weeks ago from a shelter in Jackson for their family. Emma Jo and Rachel Logan, Andy's two young *bonus* -daughters had huddled together and came out with the name *Sunshine—cause,* Emma Jo had announced, *Sunshine sounds like happy and he keeps on smiling at us.*

Mitch stepped out and shut the door. "Oh yeah, I see how you are," he yelled after the two balls of fur that quickly disappeared down the hill toward the barn. "Traitor. See if I sneak you a chicken leg!"

11

"Hey, Mitch, lose your date?" Andy greeted him with laughter as he jangled over to where Hank was already filling his plate.

"Here ya go, cowboy. Just remember, there's plenty for seconds." Hank handed him a plate already filled to overflow.

"Thanks, Hank."

"Oh, Mitch." Hank lowered his voice, arresting the cowboy's attention. "There's a pretty little single guest over there by herself. Seems a mite shy. Speak to her if you get the chance."

Mitch looked at the outline of her slender face and thick blonde curls and headed her way without so much as a glance back at Hank. It didn't dawn on him how dirty and smelly he was until he was already standing beside her table. He thought he would be doing her a big favor by walking on like he didn't see her.

But she raised her face up to look at his and dumbstruck hit him between the eyes. His heart lurched in his chest and all he could think was *I smell like cow-poop!*

"Hi. You're welcome to sit here. I was about to leave."

"Oh, uh, well I was just going to say welcome to High Point." He set his plate down and offered his hand. "I'm Mitch Corry, jack of all dude ranch stuff-to-do and cow puncher."

The warmth of his wide smile melted her into the picnic table bench. Finally, she took his extended hand and the trembling that seized her insides at that simple touch stunned her. They locked gazes for long seconds before she could find her voice—Or remember her name.

"I'm…Daisy James. Thank you, Mitch."

He released her hand and scooted onto the bench opposite her.

She didn't lie. Her plate was empty, and she *was* about to get up and wander around the grounds—but she didn't want to now. She was sure this handsome cowboy had deliberately come to sit with her. She glanced around, not finding anyone following him— like a wife or girlfriend—until the next moment a pretty woman stood up from a table where three other women and a couple of kids were seated. Carrying her plate that was still loaded with food and a cup of coffee, she stepped over the bench and plopped down beside Mitch.

"Hey, girl," Mitch grinned at her and gently elbowed her in her arm, "have you met Daisy James?"

"No, I haven't." She reached across to shake hands. "I'm Summer. Happy to meet you, Daisy."

"Thank you." She'd noticed the spurs that jangled on the heels of her boots, same as Mitch's. Oh well, a cute guy like that couldn't stay single long. *And,* she reminded herself, *that* was something she couldn't ever hope for. No man would stay and fight with the demons in her nights. That was too much to ask of anyone. Until and unless her nightmares stopped, she couldn't—she just couldn't...

Daisy stood and gathered up her paper plate and napkin. "It was great meeting you both. I'm going to walk around and see the sites before dark."

"I'll see you around then," Summer called after her. She bumped Mitch on the shoulder with the back of her hand. "She's cute. Why don't you go show her the sites?"

"Because I'm about to faint from hunger and because I stink."

She wrinkled her nose, then glanced past Mitch and back down. "So *that's* what I smell. Whew! That's a relief. I thought Hank had lost his touch."

"Lost my touch for what, Ms smarty mouth." Hank set a second plate down beside Mitch's half empty one."

"Oh my," she feigned embarrassment, "why I didn't see my all-time favorite cook standing there."

Hank gave her long dark brown ponytail a yank and hobbled off shaking his head and mumbling. "Too many sassy-mouthed women around here."

Mitch chuckled as he shoveled in another forkful.

Summer giggled. "Oh, Andy said to run by the house, and he'd give you some of the new senior feed for Tuff—See how he liked it."

"All right, I sure will. I've got his ropes in the truck, too." He turned his head one way then the other. "Where'd Andy go, anyway. He was just here."

"He grabbed a big plate and went back to the house. Rachel's not feeling well. I needed to be here to help Hank since Ms. Martha is sick in bed and all."

He nodded and shoveled in the last bite he could hold. "Thanks for the information, Summer. I better go check on old man Tuff before I head home. He worked a long, hard day for me."

"Yes, sir—and check up on that pretty little Daisy James while you're at it. She seems kind of—alone."

He grinned and cleaned up his supper trash. The fact was, he'd seen Daisy go toward the barn where his gelding was stalled. He just hated that Summer Parker was so discerning of his thoughts. He didn't know that young lady Daisy, but he thought it would be a disappointment if she wasn't at the barn. Was he really that obvious?

The barn lights were on, but it didn't appear anyone on two legs was in there. He peeled off a flake of fertilized grass hay and headed around the corner to the back row of stalls. He noticed the large pen on the side wall, that housed Jesse Brandon's cranky young stallion, had the sliding door unbolted and partially open. He froze in his tracks after his eyes adjusted to the dim lighting and he recognized Daisy James inside with her arms wrapped around the colt. The three-year-old stallion was green broke and unpredictable.

He was used to watching out for the dudes that unknowingly attempted to step into harm's way with the horses and even the campfires—but the sight of *this* woman in a position with a horse that could hurt her—or worse—stirred his adrenaline into a fierce boil.

He saw Jackson's ears perk up and then lay back nearly flat. He dropped the hay and stepped into the opening of the door. Somehow—and he couldn't say how—he grasped Daisy by her upper arm and hauled her through the small opening of the door as he jumped out backwards.

The stallion snorted and lunged at the door just as it shut, almost catching his nose.

"Easy boy. Take it easy." Mitch attempted to soothe Jackson's ruffled hair before he turned back to where Daisy had spun and was staring at him like he'd just hit her instead of saved her. He had to talk himself out of being angry at her ignorance.

When she began to rub her arm, he realized she probably felt like she'd been hit.

"I'm sorry if I hurt you, but that horse was about to do some damage that none of us would have gotten over." He stepped to her and gently caressed her bruised arm. "Maybe we should have that looked at."

"No. I'm fine. You just scared me out of a year or two. I thought I was alone and the horse seemed so gentle and..." Her eyes filled. "I didn't know horses were like that."

"Not all of them are. They're like people. Some are mean as a rattlesnake—others gentle as a lamb." He stepped to her side and placed his arm lightly around her shoulders. "Daisy, this is Jackson. He's a young stallion who hasn't been here long. He belongs to Jesse Brandon, the owner of this ranch, and still has some lessons to learn. That's why he's penned over here by himself, although most stallions are always kept apart from other horses."

He moved his arm and gathered the hay he'd dropped. "Come on, I'll introduce you to a real gentleman."

She followed his lead around the corner to a long row of stalls. When a loud whinny came from the stall she was passing, she reached out and grabbed the back of Mitch's shirt.

He would have laughed at that any other time. Instead, he stopped and grasped her hand and squeezed to calm her fear. "That's Ladybug. She's real social and gentle to ride. You'd like her."

They continued a couple stalls further. "Now, this is my best friend right here. A true gentleman and hard worker. Daisy, meet Tuff."

She pulled her hand free of his grip, feeling that he was being a little too familiar with her. He has a wife—and *this* she didn't need to ruin the trip of her life before it even got started.

15

Mitch felt his face grow warm when she pulled her hand away so sharply and stepped to place a hand on Tuff's nose. *No big deal, Mitch,* he consoled his pride. *The lady doesn't know you from Puff the Magic Dragon.*

He dropped the hay over the top of the stall and into the feeder on the inside, then stepped to the side of her and unbolted the heavy door. He slid it open and walked in first.

"Come on in. You can hug this one. He loves it."

She went in and reached out to rub the horse down his long, sweat-dried neck and giggled when he dropped his head right over her shoulder. She put her hands on either side of his neck and rubbed up and down. "Oh, you big, beautiful baby," she softly murmured against his face.

Mitch grinned at the pair of lovebirds. Women and horses—he'd seen it many times. "I hope you know this big, beautiful baby will expect this every time he sees you."

"Well then, I'll make a point to come visit him often while I'm here," she turned her face up to Mitch's, "if that's all right with you."

"Yes mam, perfectly all right. He's out working a lot of the time but catch him here and he's all yours." He nodded toward the door. "His bucket of brushes is hanging there in front of his pen. He likes that, too."

He straightened his tired back and watched her for a few seconds. "Daisy, have you ever ridden a horse?" He knew before he even asked but needed her to recognize that handling herself around a horse was different from petting a dog.

"A couple times."

He nodded. "I'll tell you what—First chance I get, I'll saddle up Ladybug for you and we'll go for a real ride."

Hastily, she stepped back out into the alleyway, not sure how to handle this. More than anything, she wanted to accept his offer. The idea of riding a horse made her want to squeal like a kid at Christmas and with this handsome cowboy who was making her heart pound in overdrive. But somehow, she doubted that Summer would appreciate his attention to her this way. He'd already held her hand a little too intimately tight and now—She just needed to throw the brakes on this whole thing.

"Thank you, Mitch…I appreciate the offer, but…I'll be riding on the trail rides scheduled for me this week. That's probably all I'll be able to handle." She hoped she sounded upbeat and appreciative of his time. She *felt* like a louse. She took in a deep breath and smiled. "Well, thanks again, Mitch. I'm sure I'll see you and your wife around some. Goodnight."

He watched her walk out, wanting to say *goodnight*—or *something*—but dern if he could get his mouth in gear before she was gone. *Wife? Wife? She thinks I have a wife? Where in the…?* Then it hit him. Summer Parker. Daisy had gotten a wrong impression of her silly friendliness at the table.

He had become close friends with Andy and Summer and their two little girls since hiring on here. But truth was, he'd known Andy for much longer.

He placed a hand on the top rail of Tuff's pen and leaned his weight into it. His other hand rested on his hip. He couldn't stop the grin from spreading across his face. He wasn't normally given to being a prankster. But this could be fun.

He turned and reached for a brush and went back inside the stall.

\*\*\*

# CHAPTER TWO

Daisy hurriedly walked to her cabin, thankful that she didn't encounter anyone on the way. It would be dark soon and she hoped being here might relieve her nightmares—*If* she hadn't created a new one for herself. Apparently, Mitch Corry is one of those flirty men who doesn't let a little thing like *marriage* get in his way.

She turned on the floor lamp and flopped down in the recliner beside it. She sighed and relaxed back in the chair and wondered how much of all that was her own doing? From the moment she saw him walking toward her, her heart somersaulted. He could have noticed her reaction to him. And what was *that* about. She'd never felt such a pull on her senses toward a man. Even now, she wished he was sitting in this cabin with her. Oddly it seemed like she had left something of great importance to her in the barn when she left from there.

She had never made room for a relationship in her realm of daily life. She went to work five days a week, out to lunch and to the movies with Kate or CeeCee; single friends from work. Then, home to her perfectly manicured yard and flower gardens. She was content with that itinerary, except for her tormented nights—the one aspect of her life that would keep her single, her nights lonely and forbearing.

But this realm of life—Mitch and Summer's world—could only be a fantasy to indulge herself in now and then. And who knows, maybe she would find out that she really didn't like this ranch living—tending to animals out in every kind of weather, freezing your backside off or drenched in sweat day in and day out, dust and poop— *and* riding horses, swimming in a hole in the creek, hay rides, eating out of a chuckwagon every day—Fat chance she wouldn't like this way of life! She'd only been here one day and the idea of going back to her mundane days and nights at home just served to depress her.

Her head sunk into the soft, mushy, leather headrest when she willed her body to relax. With her eyes closed and no quicker than it took her to sink into the chair—it began.

A picture shot into her mind and seemed to drag her backward until she saw herself in the kitchen of her childhood home and watching an older sibling trying to fend off an attack by their mother. She was pounding her head with a hot clothes iron. The cord to the iron was still plugged into the electrical socket on the wall over the countertop. Her sister never muttered a sound but jerked her arm up to her head and then away when the searing iron was smashed into the back of her hand over and over.

Daisy's throat tightened and closed over the cry that rose up until she was forced to swallow it back down. It didn't want to go down. She swallowed and swallowed and—

"Daisy?"

The deepness of the man's voice just above her head startled her. Her arm came up in a defensive move against her intruder, but when a large hand closed around her forearm, the repressed cries shot up her throat. "No! Stop!"

"Daisy, it's Mitch. Wake up."

When she opened her eyes, it was Summer's face she saw first. "Oh, honey, you were having a bad dream. We didn't mean to scare you."

Mitch let her arm go and stepped back. "We were just outside and heard you scream out. The door was unlocked, so we came in to check on you." He searched her wide opened eyes for a few seconds. "You okay?"

She nodded. "I...yes, I'm fine." She had no idea she'd fallen asleep. Embarrassment warmed her face and she quickly stood.

Summer realized how flustered she was and stepped up to try and ease the moment. "I brought you some yummy cookies my oldest daughter made today. I'll set them on the kitchen counter for you."

Thank you. Tell her thank you for me."

"I sure will, Daisy. She's into baking goodies right now— Likes to pass them around the ranch."

"Well, tell Miss Emma Jo not to forget about her favorite cowboy. I can pick mine up on my way home. They sure smell good." Mitch shifted his eyes up and down and grinned at Daisy while Summer went to set the covered plate in the kitchen.

"Oh, her daddy might argue with you on the favorite cowboy part, but she'll knock herself out making you a batch." Summer giggled. "I better head that way before she tries to use the oven without me. You know Emma Jo!"

Mitch held the door as Summer went out, then propped it fully open while he was alone with Daisy. He was realizing there was far more to this young lady than she probably intended to reveal. Maybe keeping the door wide open would make her more comfortable with him there. For some reason, he felt a need to clarify to her who he wasn't—which was a married man. Pranking her about it might be fun, but not this time. Her falling asleep and into an obvious full-blown nightmare bothered him. What in blue blazes was she fighting with? Or—who?

She stood still as though not sure what to do or say, but obviously embarrassed at being found in the throes of a bad dream.

"I would like to clear up something that you misinterpreted," he said quietly. "I'm not married. I work here and I live in the bunkhouse on the far side of the ranch."

She nodded and met his steady gaze. "I gathered that…at least, that you weren't married to Summer. It's really no big deal."

He glanced down at the floor, then back up. "It's a little bit of a deal to me. And that horseback tour of the ranch is still good if you want it."

She stared at him but couldn't form an answer. He'd just repeated his offer to take her on a personal tour—even after catching her in her most vulnerable state. She couldn't find her voice quick enough and accept his offer before he slowly turned toward the open door to leave. He stopped on the small porch and turned half way back around.

"Let me know what you decide. He stepped off the end of the step and headed toward the barn.

She went to the doorway. "Mitch?"

He stopped and turned toward her.

"I would like to take that ride. Thank you."

He grinned and tipped the brim of his dusty straw hat. "Yes, mam. I'll plan it." He continued on to the barn to check water buckets, his heart jumping like a jack rabbit on a sugar high.


Hank Walton hung up the phone in the den and gave himself a few long seconds to get control of his rioting thoughts.

"Hank, is something wrong?" Granny Martha stepped to the doorway between the kitchen and den and frowned at the tense look on her husband's face. She had already heard it in his voice.

He walked past her into the kitchen and then through to their bedroom closet. She knew as well as she knew her name what he was going to get.

"Hank Walton, you better be telling me what's going on before I call Jesse back."

He went to the kitchen and laid his shoulder holster on the table, then removed the 9mm from it before settling his gaze on his frail little wife.

"Clancy Bender escaped prison last night with two other inmates. They caught the other two, but they called Jesse to warn him that he might be headed here."

Martha raised her face heavenward. "Oh, dear Jesus, help. I guess Donny and Reeny know?"

"The whole ranch has been briefed and put on alert."

She opened a drawer in the kitchen cabinet and took out an old raggedy towel, then spread it across the middle of the table. She knew the procedure Hank followed to clean his gun. Then she turned around and began to make coffee.

He watched her for a few seconds, noticing her shaky legs and hands, before he circled the table and took her by the shoulders and firmly moved her into their tiny bedroom. "You're still sick and you're going back to bed."

When she started to protest, he gently pushed her to sit on the bed. "No, mam. Not this time. Today...I'm the boss. Now, you get under those covers and don't give me any sass."

After nearly a week of battling the flu, she was too relieved at laying still to argue. She could see him as he went back and sat at the table. She felt such love for Hank Walton at that moment—an inner pouring out of thankfulness rushing through her heart and soul for the one true love of her life. She and Hank had met on the ranch and married late in life. His nature was gentle and kind and somehow, she was allowed to be the recipient of all that sweetness. He always laughed at her jokes or her silly faces she made—whether any of it was funny or not.

Only twice could she remember seeing him this serious, even stern, and that's when he had his pistol out and his protective instinct in high gear. Both times was for the same thing—Clancy Bender.

Just the thought of that deranged monster made her cold inside.

That sweet young wife of her Donny's had been kidnapped, more like sold by her dad, on her high school graduation night. She'd been held hostage inside of a locked room in an old empty building in downtown Albuquerque—abused for months and made pregnant by that scum of the earth.

She swallowed hard at the unwelcomed memory, blinking back threatening angry tears, imagining her little Reeny girl having to endure such torture, even though God had literally sent Donny to rescue her and love her—and bring her home to the ranch.

It had been her Hank who had shot him when he brazenly came here to try and take Reeny again. They'd all thought he was dead, but God didn't see fit to let him die. He had barely survived and was sent to prison for life, for that and many other crimes.

Jesse and several others, including Donny knew the truth—that he'd survived, but Reeny wasn't told. Martha thought keeping that information from her was a mistake, but it wasn't her call to make.

She faced the door that lead into the compact kitchen, then balled up beneath the quilt and watched Hank.

He had microwaved his cup of cold, leftover coffee and sat down at the table. Methodically and without much thought, he removed the slide from the semi-automatic—then, removed the barrel and guide spring assembly. When all the parts were laid out on the towel that Martha had spread over the table, he sprayed gun cleaner and brushed and wiped each part clean. Once each piece was cleaned, he easily reassembled it—then racked the slide and squeezed the trigger to ensure all was in good working order.

About half way through the process, he turned his head to glance at his almost seventy-year-old wife. She was watching him with just her eyes and forehead showing from under the cover. He grinned at her and winked, then finished his job.

Hank had worked for High Point Dude Ranch as chuckwagon cook for well over twenty years, his identity changed years before that by the witness protection program. He hadn't let himself think about his name change in a few years.

As a rookie police officer in California, his life did a full the day he'd happened on to a huge drug smuggling ring in action and shot and killed a drug lord's gang leader son. Hank had been shot and by the time he recovered, his parents had been murdered and he was their next target. That's the day Hank Walton was born—leaving behind his true identity—Buck Rhea—and the police force, forever.

Henry and Jill Rhea. He hadn't thought of his folks in a while now, but the few times he'd needed to arm himself over the years, like today, always caused their memory to surface in vivid color. He blamed himself for the brutal way they died at the hands of a revengeful mafia gang. He was an old man now and the burden still weighed him down when the memories came, like now.

The silence was deafening, but it was the sheer look of terror on his wife's face that seared the middle of his heart.

Finally, Reeny was able to summon her voice. "Br...broke out...of prison!? But...but..." She felt like she'd been sucker punched and left to smother from lack of oxygen in the room. "I...you...said he was dead." She couldn't get above a whisper. "Hank...Hank shot him...years ago." Her eyes were large and wide and focused wildly on her husband. "Donny?"

"Reeny,..."

"No!" She threw her hands up in front of her. "No! Are you telling me you lied to me? You...you promised he would never hurt anyone again. Never come back again." Panic consumed her. "Why is he back?" Her voice was slightly lower than a squeal. "Why is he here?"

When Donny reached for her hand, she began slapping at him. Her panic was trying to graduate to shock. He stepped up closer, wrapped both arms around her and pulled her tightly against him.

"It's okay, baby. You're safe." He tightened his hold until she stopped struggling and tears began running down her face. "I'm so sorry, Reeny," he whispered over the top of her head. "I didn't mean to lie to you. He survived his wounds—We were all surprised, but he signed confessions and was sent to prison for life. By the time I found all that out, I...well, I wanted you to feel safe."

"What if he shows up here?" She pulled back from his embrace. "What if he makes it out here before they catch him?"

The terror that coated her face nearly took him down. He wasn't going to promise her there would not be a confrontation on this ranch, but he would protect her and little Donny Hank if he had to blow the man to bits himself.

"We're all going to stay at Jesse's until he's caught. Grandpa Hank and Granny Martha are coming over. Beau and Carly, too. There'll be law enforcement all over the area—even their K-9 squad."

After a silent few moments, she relaxed and stood up straighter. "I'll pack some things." She stiffly and unemotionally began pulling clothes from the dresser drawer.

He watched her for a minute. She went from being panic stricken to an angry calm. He said no more.

The baby's room was located a few steps away in their loft bedroom. Donny went in and gathered little Donny some extra changes of clothes. His little curly hair was all that was showing from beneath his covers where he was sleeping in his toddler bed and Donny had to restrain himself from scooping his son up in his arms and hold him close while he finished his nap. Paternal protective instincts rushed his blood veins with adrenalin—his metabolism high and suddenly needing something fast and furious to do—like choking the life out of that scumbag excuse for a human, with his bare hands! He had to work at calming himself enough to help Reeny get ready to go.


Laura Brandon watched a patrol car from the Jackson Hole Sheriff Department come up the drive and park alongside the patio just outside her kitchen door. She immediately recognized the tall, lanky deputy when he exited his car—The same man who had driven her to the Jackson hospital several years ago after Jesse's horse-riding accident. It had taken her a while to stop thinking about how she'd allowed her personal prayers to become audible while they traveled to the hospital, embarrassing herself in front of this stranger—One who was affected much the same way at her strange way of praying. She hadn't seen him since then, until now. Maybe he wouldn't remember, but at this point in her walk with her Heavenly Father, she was okay with whatever his reaction to her might be now.

She opened the back door just before he reached it. "Hello, Mr. Harper." Smiling.

"Evening, Mrs. Brandon." He returned a smile that showed deep in his clear blue eyes—a very different picture of him than she remembered from their last and only encounter.

"This is a good news visit, I hope?"

"Well, not yet. This convict is still on the loose. After talking to some of the other inmates at the prison, we feel sure he is heading this way." He glanced around. "Are you here alone?"

"Oh, no. Jesse is out doing evening chores and most of the family will be bunking here with us tonight…and, until he's caught. I'm sure you want to visit with Jesse. He'll be in shortly."

"Yes, I would, Mrs. Brandon." He lowered his eyes, then rested his hand on the wide gun belt around his hips.

His uneasiness wasn't lost on Laura. "Well, for starters, I'm just Laura, and if you'd like to come in, I've got fresh coffee."

"Thank you. I'll accept that as long as I'm just Mick."

She laughed. "Deal."

He followed her inside and hung his silver belly Stetson on the rack beside the door.

She pointed to the opposite side of the kitchen. "Head right in there to the den and I'll bring coffee. Sit anywhere you like."

"Actually, I'm glad we have a minute to visit…well, privately," he said after Laura served coffee and then seated herself across the small floor space from him.

She sensed what this was about. He was nervous, his adam's apple bobbing with a couple of quick swallows of saliva. She waited.

"Mrs…uh, Laura, do you remember the day I drove you to the hospital when your husband was care flighted there?"

She smiled and nodded.

"You were praying in the car…in a strange language."

"Yes, Mick, I remember it well. I hadn't meant to do that. Not out loud, anyway." Her curiosity was growing. "I'm surprised *you* remember that."

He took a swallow of coffee and set his cup on the small table beside his chair. He leaned forward with his hands clasped between slightly spread knees, then finally looked at her. "Something happened to me in the car while you were praying that day."

She slowly set her nearly full cup on her lamp table. Her mind shot backward to the few minutes before she got out of his patrol car at the hospital and recalled how he had questioned her 0about the language she was praying in. He'd cut his eyes at her, as if he *couldn't* fully look at her face.

At the time, she hadn't really understood what had happened to *her* during one of her late-night prayer times. She had felt embarrassed that she'd prayed in that Heavenly language, *other tongues,* the Bible calls it, in front of him on the drive to Jackson. But right now, her spirit was soaring, eager to hear what had happened to him that day.

She looked into his eyes. "I would very much like to hear about it."

"This may sound…well, a little crazy."

"Mick, I'm the *tongues talker,* remember." She laughed aloud. "I was crazy first. You can tell me."

He grinned and nodded his head up and down. "All right. When you got out of my patrol car, I felt almost paralyzed. I couldn't drive away for about ten or fifteen minutes. I…couldn't seem to move my body. I kept hearing some of the language you were praying. It was going over and over in my head. Then…" he swallowed hard before continuing. "Well… then I heard someone speak words in my mind. I heard, *Trust Me with all your heart and lean not to your own understanding.*"  He sat silent a moment. "Long story short, I went to church with my wife and kids for the first time two days later. When the pastor asked if anyone would give their life to Jesus Christ, I practically ran down to the front of the church." Tears streamed down the deputy's cheeks, unchecked. "I did that, Laura. I gave my life to God. I believe that prayer you were saying was partly for me. I'll never forget a second of that experience nor you." He swallowed hard and swiped at his wet face. "Thank you from the bottom of my heart."

She stood and handed him a tissue from the box on her lamp table, then pulled out another one and mopped up her own tears. "No, Mick, thank *you.* You have no idea how much I needed to hear about this. I needed a reminder of how powerful our prayers really are. I'm so happy for you and for your family."

"Thank you, mam." He stood and reached out his hand. When she reached out with hers, he covered it with both of his, holding her gaze for an extra moment with the sincerest gratitude glowing on his countenance.

Laura heard Jesse stomp the dust off of his boots just before the back door opened. He didn't take off his hat as he normally would but stalked quickly through the kitchen to enter the den. She could tell his metabolism was still revved up as it usually was when he was working.

She turned toward him when he stopped beside her. "Honey, this is Deputy Mick Harper."

Jesse stepped to him with hand outstretched. "Jesse Brandon. Glad you're here."

Mick nodded. "Yes, sir. I'm one of many. We have roadblocks from here to the state prison. We need to make sure we have all gates to this ranch guarded."

"So, you're sure he's headed this direction then?"

Mick nodded. "We have good reason to believe that. What we don't know is what he's driving. The vehicle they originally stole has been recovered along with the other two escapees."

"Let's make the rounds to my gate entrances right now. Laura, as soon as Reeny and the others get here, make sure they stay put. Period. This guy is an animal…as we all know."

"What's the status of your dude ranch guests?" Mick asked.

Jesse and Laura exchanged glances. They had already discussed with amazement, the odd timing for this to happen.

"Actually, all our guests have gone except one. No others are due here for three days. We schedule ourselves a few days to recoup and regroup once a month. Tomorrow begins that timing."

"What about the one still here?" Mick sounded like he was filling out a rote questionnaire as he and Jesse walked toward the back door.

"We have one young lady who needed this time to accommodate her vacation from work. She can hold up here with my family."

"Have you spoken to her yet?"

28

"No. She's off on a tour of the ranch with one of my hands this evening. They should be back any time." He turned in the open door and craned his neck around toward his wife. "As soon as Miss James is back, see that she moves her things in here."

"I'll watch for her and you guys please be careful."

They all heard the dually coming up the drive and Laura watched at the door until she recognized Judd Luke's vehicle. He and his foreman, Les Kane, got out and she closed the kitchen door and prayed audibly for God to take control of this situation, then she headed to the utility closet for more cots and quilts.

The ranch house filled up over the next hour. Only Carly Vance elected to stay home with her eight-month-old twin sons. The grounds were well lighted all the way around her and Beau's modular cabin and the best dead-bolts on the market secured all doors and windows. This security had been ordered by Beau's dad, Webber Vance, the day he purchased the house for his son and soon-to-be daughter-in-law just a short few weeks before his death.

Even though the house seemed relatively safe, Beau would have preferred his young family camp at the ranch headquarters. But, trying to corral two feisty early-walking toddlers in a place that wasn't fully baby-proofed—he understood Carly's argument. He would be up on a watch all night, so his house would be circled and re-circled all night under his own vigilance.

There wasn't a husband, father, grandpa or single cowboy on the ranch that wasn't outside for the night—locked and loaded. That included the neighboring Double OO folks and more law enforcement than a state wide lighted military parade.

Hank stood in the drive just outside after double checking that all doors and windows were locked down tight. He turned a slow circle as he looked over the whole ranch area as far as he could see.

"Kinda looks like Christmas around here, don't it, Hank?" Jesse walked up from the pavilion after flipping on every light he could find.

"Place looks like a little city all lit up like this." Hank pointed toward the church where the building lighted the whole hillside.

"Don't guess I've ever seen it like this. It's kinda showy." The way the elder man's eyes were shining, it was obvious he was enjoying the sight.

Jesse turned a circle. The barn and every cabin on the place was glowing inside and out. Even Andy and Summer's home, the building setting furthest away, was visible. "I believe it would be hard to hideout on this place tonight."

"I assume Miss James got settled inside the house with the others?"

Hank lifted his straw enough to scratch his head. "Well...I can't say. I haven't seen her. Come to it...I never saw Mitch this evening either."

"Go check with Laura, Hank. I'll see if their horses are in the barn." Jesse strode off to the barn.

-274    In minutes both men met at Jesse's dually beside the house, loaded up and headed toward the bunkhouse where Mitch lived.

All lights were burning inside the cabin and the small porch light was on, but only SaraLou, Clint Berry's aussie pup, was home.

"Clint is set up to watch at the east gate," Hank said.

"All right. We'll give them a little longer to show up before sending out a couple of riders to look for them." Jesse was having to hold a tight rein on his frustration at Mitch. That cowboy was at the ranch meeting to map out a plan for *this* night and until this criminal excuse for a human was apprehended. So—he'd better have a real knockout excuse for this stunt. Not to mention the one hard and fast rule of this dude ranch—no hanky-panky carrying on that would compromise the moral standard of God's Ways. There was no compromise in this. No gray area. None!

He let out a long breath and noticed Hank eyeing him a little sideways.

"Are you done stringing ole Mitch up by his...toes?"

Jesse chuckled out of pure necessity. "Yeah, for now."

"Young people today have some open-ended ways."

Before Jesse could start another rant about that, they pulled into the ranch yard and spotted Mitch and Daisy walking slowly, leading their horses toward the barn from the back pasture that led to the Honeymoon Hideout cabin. Both noticed that Mitch's aged gelding, Tuff, was stepping gently on his left front leg.

"I better go make a round. Hope that's not a serious limp," Hank said.

Jesse got out and headed for the barn. He decided to focus on Tuff for now. That horse was one of those once-in-a-lifetimers— far and few between in finding one like him. He didn't know for sure if Mitch Corry knew what he had. But for now, he needed to focus, at least a few minutes, onto something besides why Mitch was so late getting back from taking a ranch guest for a quick turn around the property or onto a vile, child rapist that the prison guards couldn't seem to keep up with.

And why, he wondered for the hundredth time, was this filth called Bender or Heinz or whatever his real name—why was he still alive on this earth?! He couldn't see a point to God allowing him to still exist and leave a possibility for someone else to be hurt. He shook his head hard, a heavy weight crushing his shoulders.

Stepping from the bright barn lights into a narrow, darkened space between the barn door and the petting zoo pens, Jesse jerked off his hat and dropped it beside his feet. He placed both hands on the side of the building and lowered his head between his extended arms, struggling inwardly to calm the anger and frustration that was trying to swallow him. He knew full well what had compromised his peace of mind. And he knew how hard it was, at times, to get it back. Once he was so full of these negative thoughts and feelings—his own mind would rather continue on that path than let go, repent and hand it back to his Heavenly Father. How many times did he have to fight through this before he stopped letting it happen? It had been three days since he'd spent time in prayer, and he knew *that* was his problem.

He felt his body relax suddenly and he seized the moment.

*Forgive me, Lord. I blow it over and over. I can't get through all this without You—without Your Mercy and Your Peace. Help me. I'll do better.*

31

After a couple of minutes waiting and focusing on what the face of Jesus looked like in his imagination—he picked up his hat, calmly put it on and entered the barn.

***

# CHAPTER THREE

He knew he was going to die. He felt it in his gut. He was obviously sick—freezing and shaking, burning with fever. He didn't care. He was at the ranch where she lived, and he also knew he would get his mission done. He had to.

Soaking wet, he made his way down the middle of the creek trying to drown his scent, figuring the prison would have the dogs after him. He hadn't heard any barking and he hoped he'd bought a little extra time by driving the old wrangler jeep he stole out of a barn some fifty miles in the opposite direction of this place. He had no idea how many miles he'd been in the creek—wading and sometimes swimming to keep his smell covered up.

Stopping in a waist deep pool, he searched the now familiar cliffs that he had camped on when he was here before. It was almost dark. He needed to find a crevice to crawl into—a rock to lay behind. He'd been in the water for hours and all he needed now was one little break. He would get to Reeny if it took his last breath.

A large tree had fallen on the opposite bank. He scrambled into the branches and climbed to the highest part to see if he could see something where he could crawl inside. Above the cliff edge, there appeared to be a shelf of rock sticking out that might serve as a cover, at least for tonight.

He hurried out of the tree and waded waist deep to the opposite side, then climbed on his hands and knees, grabbing on to small sprouting trees and brush to finally pull himself over the top. He stood up and saw the opening of a cave. It was pitch dark inside and not knowing how deep it went or what might be denned up in there, he curled up against the wall near the opening and slept, shaking with fever chills.

Mitch was squatted down examining the gelding's leg in the alleyway outside the tack room. As soon as he noticed his boss coming toward him, he immediately stood and reached his hand out as Jesse stepped up beside Tuff.

"Mitch." Jesse nodded and shook hands. "What's going on with Mr. Tuff man here."

"Well," he glanced down at the injured foot, "I think he might have dodged a bullet. He stepped in a shallow hole."

Tuff raised his foot and gingerly set it back down keeping his weight balanced on three legs.

"Mind if I take a look?"

"I would much appreciate that."

Jesse crouched beside the tender limb and examined it. "Seems like a good sprain. Watch it. If we need a vet, I'll get Les Kane to look at him." He stood, went into the tack room and came out with a bucket and tube of Bute for pain. "I'll go get some ice from the house. You'll need to run cold water over that area about every thirty minutes. Give him a little Bute Paste." He handed Mitch the medicine and turned to leave, nearly splattering himself right into the front of Daisy James.

"Whoa!", he exclaimed. "You're so quiet, I didn't hear you come up."

She smiled and quickly took a step back. "Excuse me, Mr. Brandon." She moved to stand beside Mitch. "Is Tuff going to be okay?"

"We'll see," Mitch answered. I've got to treat his ankle throughout the night." The look he settled on her was tale-telling.

It wasn't lost on Jesse. He turned around and headed to get the ice.

"I cleaned Ladybug's stall and brushed her. She's ready for supper."

He nodded. "Thank you, Daisy. I'll get Tuff to his pen and we'll feed them." He slid the tube of pain medicine into the side of Tuff's mouth, shot it in, then rubbed under his throat and neck to help him swallow it.

Daisy watched the cowboy and his horse slowly move to the back end of the barn. Her heartbeat quickened and she knew she was going to have to throw herself a reality party after leaving this place. Going home sounded bleak and boring.

She shook her head as if to derail the negative and ridiculous thoughts before she sabotaged the rest of her vacation. Instead, she would count her sweet blessings for the attention Mitch Corry was lavishing on her and accept it for what it was. This was part of his job—to entertain the guests here.

And today—despite the unfortunate injury that Tuff had suffered—had been one of the most memorable she could remember ever having. Mitch was a laugh a minute. He'd held her hand, even while they walked the horses. While they'd sat on a slab of rock on the creek bank and put their feet in the water, she knew he was about to kiss her. But she'd panicked and stood up and walked over to pet Ladybug where she was tied to a tree limb. Without a word, he'd untied her horse and helped her into the saddle. He didn't seem offended—but, mounted up and sidled his horse beside hers to take her hand. She could still feel the warmth of his large, strong palm covering hers.

"Miss James?"

"Oh!" She jumped at the near growling voice behind her and laughed, splaying her fingers across her chest. "Well, there went about five years off my life."

Jesse was slightly taken aback at the laughter that went all the way into her twinkling eyes. He couldn't hold back a grin. The joy transformed her face in such a way that she nearly looked like someone he'd never seen before. He didn't have it in him to put a damper on that with a reprimand to either her or Mitch. It appeared that Tuff may be responsible for the delay. At least part of it, anyway.

"I'm sorry, hon. Didn't mean to scare you." He headed to the back of the barn with the full bucket of ice water.

Daisy unlatched the door to the feed stall located beside the tack room and according to Mitch's earlier instruction on feeding, she scooped two rations of grain into a bucket, then pulled off two blocks of grass hay from an opened bale and with a little muscle exertion, headed for Ladybug's pen.

Jesse watched her divide the feed between both horses and fill their water buckets as if she'd done barn chores before—all while Mitch carefully soaked Tuff's foot and ankle, then massaged rubbing alcohol into the swelled area.

Once the chores were done and for the time being, Jesse needed to get his only dude ranch guest into a safe place for the night.

"I assume Mitch explained something of our situation here with an escaped convict in our area?"

"Yes, sir, he did."

"All our womenfolk and children are staying together in mine and Laura's house tonight. My wife has a bed fixed for you, too."

She knew there was no way she could chance sleeping in a house full of people—chance disrupting their sleep with one of her nightmares.

Mitch could see the turmoil of thoughts she was having. "I think she had planned to help me out with Tuff during the night— soaking his foot. I've got to head to the east gate to help Clint." He motioned his hand toward Daisy. "If that's all right with you, Jesse."

Jesse looked from one to the other, not real sure what to think, but simply nodded. "Alright...well, you two work it out. Somebody will make a round through here periodically." He gave Mitch a *watch yourself* glance before he turned and left the barn.

Mitch understood, but with just a twinge of malice. He had to remember this was his work place and that slight warning came from the owner of this ranch—his boss. And he had been given the rules of conduct the day he hired on. Still, at his age, it felt a little like a parent/child admonition. But—he would adhere because

Jesse and Laura Brandon's rules demanded morality according to God's ways and *that* he truly understood.

He remembered the moment that Jesus Christ became his Savior just a few short years back. His little praying mama had walked a quarter of a mile out into the pasture where he was sitting on Tuff and crying like a baby. It happened all of a sudden—One minute he was heading out to work and the next, he'd stopped his horse and tears were running like an open faucet, his whole insides feeling like the worst sinner ever born. Guilt ridden with his shoulders bent under some unseen force, he'd caught sight from the corner of his eye of his mother walking briskly toward him. She wore jeans, boots and her faded green checkered apron tied around the waist of a pink T-shirt—a sight he would remember even after he was dead and gone, he felt sure.

When she had reached him, she'd patted his leg and tilted her head back to look at his wet streaked face. *Git down son. My neck's going to get a crick if I have to talk to you this way.*

He'd dismounted, still bawling. She simply said, *The Lord just told me to come out here to you because your heart was calling to Him and it was your time to get saved. Are you ready to pray? I'll help you."* His mother was never one to beat around the bush.

He could only nod his head up and down. She began to cry, too, and the next thing he knew, he was blubbering out a prayer as his mom, choking back sobs, led him in the right words.

*Whew, that 'come to Jesus dust' He throws down is powerful stuff, huh, son,* she had said as she tried to get control of her emotions.

They had both dissolved in laughter at that. She'd insisted on walking back to the house and all Mitch remembered afterward about that day was when he mounted up again, he had felt like he only weighed about 10 pounds. Nope, he'd *never* forget that day!

"Mitch?"

He jerked slightly when a hand suddenly touched his forearm.

"Are you all right?"

He realized a tear was trickling down his face. He grinned and swiped at it. "I'm better than fine, pretty girl. I was just thinking about my mom."

"Does she live around here?"

"No, my parents moved on to Heaven a while back."

"Oh! I'm sorry."

"Don't be. They're together and living well up there." He smiled and motioned upward with his thumb.

She studied the fondness that glistened on his face while speaking of his parents—particularly his mom. "Your mother was really good to you, wasn't she?"

Her question gave him pause as he kept his gaze on her face. "Absolutely she was. Mama's are a special breed of people. They'll fight a circle saw if it threatens one of their babies. Mine was a prayer warrior—Took on the devil himself for my soul. And…she won.!" He shook his head and chuckled.

A slight smile pulled her lips. Her emotions were a jumbled mixture while she worked to show the positive ones. "What a special lady. I wish I could have met her."

He wanted to ask her about her family—wanted to know *everything* about her. But he needed to get out to the east end of the ranch and join Clint on the night watch that he was asked to do. He needed to fix his mind on a demonized escaped prisoner who would possibly be looking for a way into this ranch. And here—in this barn—with this woman—wasn't going to get that job done.

"Thank you, Daisy. She *was* special. I've got to get to work now. The ice is in bags in the freezer there in the tack room. Me and Tuff appreciate your help. If you need anything, Jesse, and I think, Mr. Walton, the ranch cook, will be within yelling distance outside. Okay?"

"Yes. You go. I'll be fine with this."

He tipped his hat, turned on a heel and left. The night was quiet outside, but he knew the place was crawling with law officers and cowboys, all legally locked and loaded. He checked his firearm that was concealed under a thin wrangler vest that he wore for that purpose, then stepped up into the cab of his pickup and headed through the well-lighted ranch yard to the dark pasture.

More than ever, he wanted to know about Miss Daisy James. There was no mistaking the pain in her eyes when she'd asked if his mom was good to him. Who even thinks of something like that—unless her young life was—not so good? There was something in the way she had looked at him when she'd asked the question. Pain, yes. But—deeper than that. He had the feeling she was struggling with wanting to talk about something. The nightmare he had witnessed while she was napping a couple days ago rolled through his mind, but then he pushed it aside and forced his attention on the job he was out here to do tonight. He decided to give her the first couple hours of tending his pony's foot, then he'd take over and come and go the rest of the night.

Daisy had treated Tuff's foot twice now. It had been nearly an hour since Mitch left. She twisted the irritating watch band back and forth on her wrist. With no cell service here, a timepiece was one of the things listed on her *Things to Bring* sheet that was mailed to her along with her reservation confirmation.

She took a seat on the bale of hay setting outside the tack room door, glad of the gentle feel of the barn full of horses. A snort here and there, a bucket banging against the stall wall. For the first time, she realized a radio was playing—the low vibrations coming from just above her head. She craned her neck to see a small radio high on the side wall of the feed area. She recognized the oldie, but Country Music goodie—Only Make Believe by Conway Twitty. She grew up on these old country songs. They were her *go to* when the world got too hard to live in—which was almost daily.

With her eyes closed, imaging herself dancing a two-step with Mitch down the concrete alley of the barn, she jumped at the feminine voice in front of her.

"Daisy, I brought you some supper." Laura held a foil covered bowl in one hand and a thermos bottle in the other. "And coffee."

The food smelled delicious. Daisy suddenly realized she was starving. She scooted to one end of the hay, took the bowl and set it beside her. Laura propped the thermos on the floor against the bale.

"Thank you so much, Mrs. Brandon. Smells like heaven."

"It's my specialty...chicken and dumplings. And there's plenty more. Jesse delivered dinners to all the hands where they are standing guard tonight, but I made a huge caldron of this...so don't hesitate to come to the kitchen and get more. Jesse or Hank will be checking on you." She reached into one of the deep pockets on her apron and pulled out a sealed packet containing a plastic fork, knife and spoon. "Oh, here ya go. I almost forgot this."

"Thank you."

Laura couldn't pinpoint what was bothering her about Daisy James, but something like a heaviness had settled in her spirit the moment she saw her sitting on the hay bale with her eyes closed. *Lord, is there something I need to do here...to say to this young girl?*

Her Father wasn't giving up any information, so she made a mental note to pray for her more tonight.

"I have an extra bed made for you if you want to sleep a few hours."

The look Daisy gave her was one of uncertainty or confusion.

"Mitch *did* tell you about—"

"Yes, mam. He did...but...I would like to stay out here and take care of Tuff tonight."

Laura nodded. She couldn't talk now with the huge lump that formed suddenly in her throat. She felt the Spirit of God calling her to pray for something or someone. Maybe Daisy. But she bent over and patted her on the knee, then quickly left.

Every room in the house had cots and pallets and people, so she headed for the rental cabin directly across from the house and went inside so she could have some privacy. As fast as she closed the door behind her, she dropped to her knees and allowed the Holy Spirit to pray through her. Tears began to flow immediately as a heavy burden for someone, somewhere came on her. A Heavenly language poured from her mouth for several minutes. Then it all stopped as suddenly as it had begun.

She had no idea who her prayer burden was for, but she left that with the Lord and got up and went home.

Nearly three hours later, Laura peeked into each area where kids and moms were in bed before she lowered the kitchen lights and headed for bed.

Granny Martha was on a half bed that had been set up in fourteen-year-old Anna Leigh's room. Martha was feeling much better after her few days bout with the flu, so she shared the room with Anna Leigh and Emma Jo Logan. Little Rachel opted for a thick quilted pallet alongside her mom, Summer.

Laura felt like "Mama Brandon' tonight—responsible for all the warm bodies sleeping under her roof. It wasn't a bad feeling, but not one that was going to let her sleep much. *That,* plus the fact of all the family men, including law enforcement and ranch cowboys up all night in a possible dangerous situation.

She left her T-shirt and jeans on in case she needed to get up quickly in the night—piled pillows against the headboard and let her head sink down into them. Again—she prayed for all on the night watch and for a quick end to this sordid circumstance.

A minute later, she heard Jesse's voice.

"Laura? Honey?" He whispered.

Why was he whispering at her? She turned her head toward the bedroom door and looked at him, then he came in and closed the door.

"Jesse, is everything all right?"

"Yes, mam, it is. I was just checking on everybody in the house."

"We're all fine. I just laid down."

He laughed. "You did, huh. I've been in here twice tonight and you never knew it. I woke you this time because I was coming in for a few minutes and I didn't want to scare you with that hog-leg I know you've got under one of those pillows."

She looked at him like he had a second head, making him laugh again. "What time is it?"

"Three a.m."

"What?"

He lay down beside her and draped a long arm around her, then dragged her against him into that perfect spoon where she always fit so well. "One of the deputies is in the yard with Hank. That old man has got more stamina than most twenty-year-olds. Couldn't get him to take a break...even a couple of hours." He was talking with his forehead against the back of her head, his eyes closed. Her hair always smelled like fresh air.

"Did Daisy come in here to sleep?" she asked.

"Uh uh. Mish... came... to the..." An easy snore finished whatever he was saying.

She smiled and rubbed the hairy arm that encircled her waist. She knew whatever Daisy and *Mish* Corry did for the night—Jesse was comfortable with it. He was out cold.

Within seconds, so was she.

After two days of this tight security routine, there had been no sign of the escaped convict anywhere. It seemed he had vanished from the state.

The family had been called to a meeting in the ranch office where the Marshall was updating them on what little he knew. This was not good news to any at High Point and Donny was especially rankled at the whole situation. He felt all eyes following him across the room and out the door. He refused to hear any more of what this man had come to tell them.

His wife had been kidnapped and victimized by the scum bag for months until she was able to escape by an unlocked door and then jump into his dually to hide. That's how he and Reeny had met and soon fell in love.

A flash of emotion built up in his chest until he desperately wanted to kill the man. They thought he was dead after being shot by Hank when he'd brazenly come here and tried to kidnap Reeny right off this ranch.

Donny clenched his hands into tight fists as he headed for his pickup and drove out of the ranch yard and toward the canyons. His mind was running in high gear—out of control.

Reeny's father, if that's who he really was, literally sold her and set up her kidnapping the night she graduated high school. Then the pervert locked her away, raped her, got her pregnant and had the evil nerve to show up at this ranch to steal her back.

The memories brought bile rushing up his throat, making him cough and groan with more anger and revulsion than he'd ever felt in his life. To top all this off—What this must be doing to his precious Reeny—knowing *he* had lied—by omission, but, lied to her about the fact that this despicable trash had not died from his gunshot wounds. He lived and was sent to prison for life for many crimes including his murderous involvement with some mafia bunch of hoodlums. It had been agreed to leave Reeny out of the legal proceedings—to tell her nothing, not even that he was alive.

And today, she left Jesse's house and took Donny Hank home, refusing to speak to him. If that wasn't enough—that U.S. Marshall sits in the ranch office and dares to tell a story about inmate Clancy Bender having claimed his soul was saved by Jesus Christ in his jail cell!

It was too much for Donny. If the likes of *that* could be found walking the streets of gold—he'd have to pass. What a joke! He hit the steering wheel with his fist so hard, he thought he'd broken at least one of his fingers. He didn't care. The pain almost felt good—helping to ease the pain that was about to blow the top of his head off!

He hit the steering wheel again and lost his breath for a few seconds when the same finger took the hit. It took a full minute to fight down the nausea the excruciating pain created. He'd destroyed the one thing that Reeny needed above everything—to know that there was someone in the world who would not lie to her or deceive her in any way. Once trust is broken, you don't ever get it back. How could he have let this happen to her!?

He stopped, jerked the truck in park and turned the engine off. After a minute, he jumped out and walked briskly through the pasture and into the canyons close to where Jesse had been thrown off his horse and broke his leg a few years ago. With his insides in a screaming uproar, all he could do was walk fast and try to assuage some of the rage he was feeling. This wasn't like him and he hated the murderous thoughts bombarding his mind. How dare this evil, heinous, rotten to the soul piece of scum even speak the name of Jesus!

He stopped a minute and squatted down, covering his face with his hands. The blood rushing through his veins like a white-water rapid jumped him back to his feet. He slung his head back, his eyes searching to see into the heavens. "Why!?" He shouted. "Why did you let him live!? Hasn't she been through enough!?"

Somehow the outburst seemed to take the edge off of his raw nerves. He felt his body begin to relax, his shoulders slumped as his face lowered to stare at the ground. He felt numb as he took a few steps to the base of a large pine tree, sat down and let his body collapse against it. Fifteen seconds later—he fell asleep.

Reeny was relieved to hear that she and little Donny Hank could sleep in their own beds at home. She had no complaints about the past two nights on a cot that Laura had made so comfortable with a mound of quilts. If she felt anything at all, it was well loved by this entire family and ranch hands here. They had all worked tirelessly to keep her and her family safe, *but*— and she knew there shouldn't be any *buts* —even if the others here didn't know the truth—that Clancy Bender was alive and in prison—Donny should have told *her*. Instead, everyone here knew the truth, *except* her! It was her husband's responsibility to tell her the truth. What else is he keeping from her? The trust she'd had in Donny Brandon was without a fault. Whatever he said was fact. Whatever he didn't say—never happened. He was her savior—almost God to her. And now this perfect trust was broken. Shattered.

Donny stumbled through the woods. It was dark and the weird night sounds were something he'd never heard before—like a wailing or moaning in the wind. He hated the sounds, but he kept walking. He needed to get home where it was safe, and he could sleep. He wasn't sure suddenly of the direction he was going. Tree limbs popped and scraped his face—he stumbled over a bush, barely staying on his feet. Those ungodly sounds were louder now. Finally, he entered a clearing and saw it. The wails and moans were coming from a mangy stray hound. He was laying on his side with all four legs stretched out, trembling from head to tail and obviously very sick. He approached the dog. "I'll help you, old fella." On closer inspection, he had open sores all over him and raw skin where mange had infected him. He reached to comfort the dog with a touch to the side of his face when it partially raised up and viscously bit Donny's hand. Jerking back, he saw his skin dangling in shreds from the bite, but oddly, there was no pain— only great compassion for the poor helpless mutt. He simply gathered him up in his arms, his own blood from his hand mingling with the animal's wounds. *It's all right. I'll help you get free of your pain.* He began to run, carrying the growling, snapping dog like a baby in his arms through the darkness. He knew he was headed for Les Kane's house, the Double OO foreman and local veterinarian. Suddenly he was on Les's front porch. The front door opened, but it wasn't Les standing there. It was Reeny. He no longer held the dog—but a folded sheet of paper. He handed it to her.

Donny woke up, realizing immediately that he was calm— peaceful. Apparently, he had been asleep several hours. It would be dark soon.

When he pushed against the ground with his smarting finger, he moaned from the sharp shooting pain. The sound of his agony reminded him of the pitiful dog in his dream. He recalled every detail, but as dreams so often are, there was no sense to it. He stood, swayed slightly from his deep sleep, then headed for his truck, wondering why the sick dog had turned into a sheet of paper.

\*\*\*

# CHAPTER FOUR

Daisy had sat up and tended to Tuff's injured foot until around 2am two nights ago but retired to her cabin when she couldn't convince Mitch that she truly wanted to finish out the night helping with his pony. He had walked her to her cabin, double checked all windows and locked the front door on his way out—after he stood as close as he could get facing her and wrapped his large warm hand around the side of her neck. He searched deep into her wide, admiring eyes for several long seconds, smiled at whatever he was seeing, then turned and left.

She sucked a deep breath, bouncing back and forth between disappointment that he didn't kiss her and elation at the emotional, caring expression he had conveyed from his eyes into hers. Never had anyone looked at her like that—like he truly *saw* her and liked what he saw. She wanted to chase him down and fling herself into his arms—beg him to finish out the night in her bed. But she just wrapped her arms around herself and envisioned that tender gaze he'd seared her with until she showered and fell exhausted into bed.

The warmth and genuine affection Mitch had seen, as deeply as he could get into the window of her soul, had stirred him in such a way that sleep couldn't compete with the affirmation she left him with for the rest of that night.

He had let Tuff rest and headed back out to scan the area on the east side of the ranch. He had relieved Clint Berry, insisting that he go to the bunkhouse and sleep a few hours. He was too fired up inside to feel tired—thanks to a little blonde headed girl who had managed to send his heart into a dizzy spin.

He sensed that she desperately needed him. And that alpha to-the-rescue part of him wanted to run back to her cabin and wrap her up in his arms—while his wilder, single, no responsibilities but himself part wanted to never enter the ranch yard again until she had gone home to Texas.

But that was two nights ago. He hadn't laid eyes on her since locking her cabin door behind him that night—choosing to accept day work on the Double OO for ranch foreman, Les Kane. He needed to clear his head and stop his heart from taking such a major turn. But—it didn't work. *Daisy James. Daisy James.* God help him, he was done for.

The ranch remained on high alert with police officers stationed at the gates and on patrol particularly around Donny and Reeny's house around the clock.

Hank Walton, Jesse, Donny and all the hands had taken a turn each night for a two-hour watch, walking and riding certain perimeters in addition to all the law enforcement. Nothing out of the ordinary had been seen.

The Brandon's hadn't taken any new dude reservations during all this drama. Daisy was the only guest and they had left it up to her to stay or return home and reschedule at a later time. But, knowing that the usual schedule of hay rides, trail rides, big weekly wing-ding in the pavilion would be canceled, she convinced them she was just happy to be in Wyoming in a cabin/teepee and taking a horseback ride when possible.

Mitch had spent a couple of extra-long days at the Double OO—heading out before dawn and returning to the bunkhouse after dark. But the hard work didn't help him get to sleep before spending hours fantasizing about Daisy first.

He had grabbed a can of soup and crackers from the bunkhouse for supper two nights in a row. Today, he was starved. But he showered and put on clean clothes before heading over to devour Hank's chuckwagon fare—and see Daisy James.

He spied her sitting alone on the patio just inside the open gates beside the hot tub. It was rare to see the end gates open, as it also exposed the back door into the ranch house leading into the Brandon's kitchen.

"Hey, cowboy," Hank grinned at him when he held out his plate to be filled with beef brisket, mashed potatoes and beans— but he was clearly focused the opposite direction toward the hot tub patio. "Pretty red umbrella over there, huh, Mitch?"

He grinned and cut Hank a sideways look. "That she is. That she is."

"Well, hold that plate upright before you go and embarrass yourself."

He grabbed the overfilled Styrofoam platter with both hands while Hank stuck a plastic knife and fork into the potatoes to hold them.

Mitch saw her glance up to see him coming, but she quickly turned her head away. That non-greeting was a deserved snub. He figured this might take a little effort to get her over her irritation at him. Actually, this could be a good sign—She must have missed him.

"Hello, young lady. Mind having some company?" He put his plate on the table and pulled out the chair directly across from her, rather than taking one beside her.

"Hi, Mitch." She didn't answer his question but smiled and nodded.

"I...suppose you've been finding plenty to stay entertained around here?" He asked.

She smiled and sipped her tea. He noticed she hadn't started eating. He also noticed she was dressed in a sexy little pink sundress—her curly blonde hair was even more sexy than the dress and her pink lips and cheeks matched her dress. He'd never seen her so beautiful. Had she dressed this way hoping he would be here tonight?

"Yes, as a matter of fact, I've barely had time to catch a breath."

Did he hear a little snippy attitude in her voice?

48

"Being the lone guest has had its perks. Everyone has gone out of their way to make sure I'm enjoying my stay here. I guess you've been real busy yourself?"

He fought back the rush of guilt that wanted to slide into him. And he really didn't know what he had to feel guilty about. He knew he had deliberately avoided coming to the ranch yard, even for supper, because of the feelings for her that he did *not* want to have. He just needed to apologize and start this whole thing over again.

"Look, Daisy...I..."

Her eyes moved past him then and she smiled at someone who had apparently come up behind him, cutting off his attempt to fix his mess-up.

He twisted his upper body around to see AJ White, one of the older hands for the Double OO standing behind him holding a plate of food and a drink. The only thing was—he was dressed like he had some place special to go—same as Daisy.

He set his dinner down on the table and extended a hand. "Hey, Mitch." They shook hands. "Mind if I butt in. I'm starved." His drawl was low and gravelly. "Sorry, Daisy. I'm running a little late. I warned you that might happen."

"It's no problem, AJ. Mitch was kind enough to keep me company."

AJ was several years older than Mitch—cowboy to the bone and hard working. He'd worked off and on, mostly on, for the Double OO, making the ranch bunkhouse his home for a number of years and preferring to be astride a horse from dawn til dusk. He had to be around forty years old, but his leathery tanned skin made him look much older. He was a gentle and unassuming soul who didn't have a bad word in him—but was tough as boot leather and didn't have an enemy to call his own. Every Sunday morning without fail, AJ stood beside the front door of the church and greeted each person with a smile and a handshake. Every man, woman and kid that came to church out here knew AJ.—And loved AJ.

But right at this moment, Mitch was not feeling the love—or the appreciation of what he was apparently seeing. AJ was dressed in his Sunday best, including the silver belly Stetson he wore just on Sundays.

When he made a move to get up and let him and Daisy have the privacy they'd seemingly dressed for, AJ dropped a heavy hand on his shoulder.

"Keep your seat, Mitch. There's plenty of room. Me and this beautiful little lady are going to tour Jackson Hole, but that's not til later."

Mitch settled back in his chair while he rested a slow look on Daisy that was filled with questions and mixed emotions. Suddenly he felt a little sick, his appetite gone.

His peripheral vision caught Beau Vance carrying both arms loaded with food trays while Carly pushed a twin stroller full of towheaded double trouble behind him. They were headed for the pavilion. He grabbed an excuse for himself.

"There goes the man I need to see." He pushed his chair back and scooped up his plate and drink. "Excuse me and enjoy your evening." He nodded at Daisy and walked off toward the picnic tables.

She watched him go and when she looked back at AJ, he was eyeing her with a knowing squint in his eyes.

She tipped her head toward his plate. "Don't let that good food get cold."

"I won't if you won't."

For the sake of saving face, Mitch went straight over and greeted the Vance family, shaking hands and rubbing the toddler boys on top of their thick heads of hair.

After only a minute of that, he dumped his still full plate and cup into the trash barrel, headed for his truck and drove out. In afterthought, he knew he should have, at least, taken the food back to the bunkhouse, but too late now. He kept his eyes straight ahead as he passed the patio where Daisy and AJ were eating under a big red umbrella.

Daisy couldn't help but glance up at his pickup as it went by, a stab of pain piercing her heart. She had missed him terribly the past couple of days. She wondered if he had cleaned up for her benefit before coming over to eat.

"Daisy, hon, if you'd rather," AJ drawled, "we can tour the town another time." He smiled knowingly under his salt and pepper mustache. He was as bone thin as he was tall and Daisy found that she was enjoying his easy, slow company, despite the confusion in her heart.

She met his grin with a genuine twinkling smile. "AJ, *hon,* I am looking forward to this night to...prowl or...color the town...or..."

He laughed out loud and reached for one of her hands—swallowing it between his oversized palms and long fingers. "Just for future reference, its night to howl and paint the town—and I swear, Daisy James, if I wasn't old enough to be your daddy, I'd be on a mission to catch your heart." He got up and helped her up. "Come on...lets go do some *prowling* and *coloring* before this old man's bedtime catches up to him." He was still chuckling as they walked to his truck.

Daisy laughed too, thinking how lucky she would have been to have had a daddy like AJ White.

Before they could drive out, Laura waved for AJ to stop and roll down his truck window.

"Yes mam, what can I help you with, Miz Brandon?"

She stepped off of the back steps from the kitchen and went up to the window. "Hello, AJ. Daisy. Wondered if you've seen Donny this afternoon. He left here a little upset early today and Reeny called looking for him."

He squinted, creasing his forehead as he stared briefly out the front windshield before shaking his head. "No mam, I don't recall seeing him at all today."

She took a step back. "Okay, no problem. Thank you, AJ." She wondered for only a fleeting second where he and Daisy were headed looking so spiffy. "He'll show up soon." She waved as they

51

drove off, then headed to the pavilion to check with Beau Vance and others who were in for supper.

Fiery emotions wretched through Mitch as he drove down the highway, too fast. He knew he was acting like a school boy and out of character for him. He slowed down on a clear straight area of the road and made a quick U-turn. He was being ridiculous, and he knew it. What had he expected her to do while he snubbed her, trying to decide if he wanted to pursue a relationship with her? The lady obviously had some deeply embedded emotional problems and she needed somebody—some *stable-headed* somebody—to help her. He needed to pull his head out and focus on what he knew deep down inside—that he had some part to do in helping this girl. She was traumatized. Those nightmares seemed to be lying in wait for her to dare to close her eyes and sleep. He knew that's why she was so adamant about not sleeping at the Brandon's house with everyone else and why he helped her to not have to do that.

Just then, he recognized AJ's truck as he and Daisy drove past him headed for town. He heard the horn blare, so he stuck up his fingers that were clasping the steering wheel. The tint on AJ's windows prevented him from seeing inside the truck clearly, but he could make out two shadowy figures inside as they passed by. At least she wasn't sitting close beside him.

He drove back to the bunkhouse. He'd go visit her later tonight.

Donny parked along the side of his log house and sat in the truck for a few minutes. It looked like every lamp in the house was burning on both floors. Reeny liked lamp light. She said it made the house more romantic and cozier. He smiled. There weren't less than fifteen lamps of every size and shape in that house, as well as on the back patio. She was great at making their house a home— clean and nice smelling with candles and such. And little Donny Hank had the best mom in all of Wyoming. She loved that little boy—Made sure he knew he was well loved. Reeny hadn't known a day of real love in her young life—not until Donny. And he loved that lady so much, it was soul-crushing to think of how he had hurt her.

His eyes filled and he swallowed fast and hard. He could go in there and apologize until dawn but doubted he could restore the trust he'd destroyed. He meant well. God knew he did. He meant to protect her—to see to it that she didn't spend her time looking over her shoulder in fear of that filth Bender coming back. He let her believe he was dead and gone forever. Bender should have been dead. He deserved to be dead.

He got out and headed toward the front of the house. Before he reached the porch, the front door opened and Reeny rushed out and stopped on the edge of the foot-high porch. Her eyes were large and anxious.

Donny stopped and while their eyes met and locked together, every conceivable horror shot through his mind. Was something wrong with their son? His brother, Jesse?

"Reeny, honey? What is it?"

"He's dead. His body was found today here on the ranch."

"Bender?"

She nodded her head, then stepped slowly down the porch steps and into her husband's arms. As soon as his arms wrapped around her, she burst into tears and sobbed into his chest.

He tightened his hold and splayed a hand over the back of her head, pressing her securely to him. He held her silently, letting her cry it out.

Finally, when she pulled back enough to raise her eyes up to his, she saw pain etched across his face like she hadn't seen before. Even in the darkness, the yellow light from the porch cast a golden glow on his weary features, touching her emotions deeper than she'd ever felt. Her heart hurt for her Donny. She knew she was to blame for what she saw.

"I'm so sorry, Donny. I understand why you didn't tell me the truth. I really do. You didn't deserve the way I treated you." This man—her man—had been nothing but a total offering of himself to her from the day she had jumped into his truck to hide from her perverted captor. He had protected her from that day and showed her what it was like to be truly loved—right up to this moment. The love she felt for Donny Brandon was exploding her heart into pieces.

"I never meant to hurt you, Reeny." He cupped her face and clearly saw the true emotions of her love twinkling through her tears. "My baby girl," he whispered as he kissed her lips gently. His heart was full, and he internally thanked his Lord Jesus.

"Donny, you should go see Jesse. He's been looking for you."

"I guess the baby's asleep?"

She nodded. "You can tell me everything when you get back."

He kissed her lips again. "I will tell you all I find out." He turned and climbed back in his truck.

A county patrol car was parked in the drive beside Jesse's house. He hurried inside through the kitchen door, eager to find out the details.

"In here, brother," Jesse called out.

Mick Harper stood and shook Donny's hand when he entered the den. He was the deputy who had kept the family informed throughout this nightmare. He was also the one Donny had stormed out on earlier that day.

"Donny, I'm glad you made it here tonight. If you'll have a seat, I need to fill everyone in on things."

"Okay." He sat next to his brother on the short sofa while Laura occupied her chair across from them. "I'd like to offer an apology to all of you for acting like an idiot this morning."

"Far as I'm concerned, son, you owe me nothing," Deputy Harper said. "You and that little wife of yours have been through a lot on account of that one man. This whole family has. So, think nothing of it."

Jesse patted his brother's knee as Laura nodded toward him. "That's right, Donny," she said.

The deputy spoke directly to Donny. "I'm assuming you know that Mr. Bender's body was found today?"

He nodded. "Where exactly?"

"Up on top of a ledge above the creek just to the north of here."

Donny squinted at him and sat up straighter. He glanced at Jesse. "That's where the cave..."

"He wasn't in the cave," Jesse quickly cleared that up. "He was up above on the top of it. It didn't appear that anyone had been inside."

The thought that he could have been in the same spot that little Bonnie was born and died would have been too much to deal with. He looked at Jesse again, needing further verification.

"I looked up there myself, brother. It appeared he had lain out on the ledge by the cave entrance, but never entered it. His body was found up higher in the open."

"What killed him?"

"We figure he suffered a heart attack or some illness," the deputy answered. "Course we can't be sure til the autopsy results come back. There was no obvious trauma to the body."

"Okay. So, I guess that's, that?" Donny was anxious to get back to Reeny.

"Well, not exactly. There is something that we found on him— stuffed inside his shirt."

"Something to do with my wife?"

"Yes, sir. It's a letter written to her. She doesn't know about this yet. We decided to get your opinion about how to go about this with her—under these sordid circumstances of her past with him."

It was a minute before Donny could find his voice. "Let me see it."

Deputy Harper opened his clip board and drew out a folded sheet of wrinkled paper. He leaned forward and handed it to him."You're the only one besides me and the Sheriff who has seen this."

Donny quickly unfolded the paper and read it.

*To the girl, I am unworthy to speak your name so I can only pray to God that this letter finds its way to you. I pleaded for the prison warden to take this message to you, but understandably, I was refused. So I will try with my last hours on earth to get it to you to tell you the sorrow I feel for what I did to you. I cannot ask you for forgiveness. The vile actions I committed against you are unforgivable and I will stand before Almighty God to be rightly judged. I asked Jesus to forgive me, but I could only feel the intense evil of my sin. Death is my reward. I welcome death. I am sorry I am sorry.*

He stared in disbelief at the paper in his hands. There was no denying what had happened to Clancy Bender behind those prison bars. Saying his emotions were mixed didn't come close to the turmoil popping his nerve endings. He knew, no matter what, he *had* to give this letter to Reeny. He leaned forward and handed it to Laura.

She took it and sat back to read.

No one spoke while Laura silently, thoroughly scanned the page. When she finished, she glanced up at Donny and then Jesse with tears brimming. She grabbed a Kleenex and quickly dried her eyes before handing it back to Donny.

Next, Jesse read it and then laid it on his younger brother's lap.

Laura broke the ensuing silence, her voice just above a whisper. "This man met Jesus before he died. His repentance was heartfelt, and he was desperate for Reeny to know the depth of his remorse."

Donny rubbed both hands up and down his face trying to get a grip on his rising anger. "Do you...does anybody know how sickening this is to me?"

"Little brother...everybody in this room feels disgust. That's our human nature demanding justice for our Reeny. Humanly speaking—we don't want that man to repent and wind up in Heaven. But I know that you know God Almighty forgave him— even *loved* him *before* he repented."

Laura slowly bobbed her head up and down. "Only God knows what happened in his younger life that may have driven his behavior someway." She paused a moment. "I don't know why, but I keep envisioning Mr. Bender as a poor old hound dog that's all bloody—nearly beaten to death."

Donny slowly raised his head and stared big-eyed at his sister-in-law. Then his mouth dropped slightly open and he stared into space.

"What is it, Donny?" Laura thought maybe she should have kept that to herself.

"I dreamed that—what you just said." Suddenly he jerked up the sheet of paper. "And this?" He stared at the letter in his raised hand, then slowly lowered his arm as full recognition hit him.

Relaxing with a fresh easiness settling in his mind, he related the events of his angry excursion into the canyon and then detailed the dream he had. "And when Reeny opened Les's front door, the wounded dog suddenly turned into a sheet of paper. I handed her the paper. Then I woke up."

All mouths were now open, taken aback at Donny's story.

Deputy Harper leaned forward, his forearms resting on his knees. "You know, in my profession, I've heard a lot of wild stories from people, but this is one that literally makes the hair on my arms stand up. It's like I'm sitting here actually watching God Almighty work right in front of my face!" He shook his head. "I don't know what to say, but…I feel a need right now to go home to my family. You all need time to be together. Donny, is there anything I can do where Ms. Reeny is concerned?"

Donny shook his head. "No, thanks, but I need to go and see my own family right now."

The deputy left and Donny went out behind him.

After looking in on their sleeping brood, Jesse and Laura prepared for bed without any more talk. They each seemed to have the same idea—the same need to just be quiet.

Jesse waited for Laura to settle under the bed covers, then he turned the lighted clock upside down on the floor beside his bedside table to extinguish its light—clicked off his lamp and slid into bed. He took his bride of over twenty years into his arms. Here's were already reaching for him in the pitch darkness and as soon as they pulled themselves close together, Laura let the tears loose that were crowding her throat.

Jesse knew this was coming and Laura knew he was making a darkened little safe haven for her to let down. She always liked him to hold her in the dark when she was emotional. It was one of those little things he'd learned early on about her. These effusive times didn't happen too often these days but recognizing it when it did happen had become second nature. He didn't say a word but let the warmth and strength of his arms and hands caress and soothe to convey his love. And he *did* love this woman. Nothing and no one on earth took precedence over her.

After a while, Laura pulled back and sucked a deep breath. Jesse loosened his hold but waited for her to demand more space. He kissed her forehead and smoothed her hair. "I love you, you know. In fact, I'd ask you to marry me, Mrs. Brandon, if I thought you would even consider it." He could feel her smiling in the darkness.

"One of these days, Mr. Brandon, I'm going to surprise you and take you up on it."

He leaned down and kissed the top of her head. "Well, in that case, we could get some practice in…I mean…while we're here…like this…and all."

"Jesse?"

"Huh?"

"Shut up."

She raised up and pushed him onto his back and kissed his laughing mouth, then squealed as he flipped her over and under him in one effortless move.

Reeny was patiently waiting downstairs when Donny arrived home. She had showered and slipped into a knee-length white lounging shift that she sometimes slept in.

He was glad she hadn't settled in bed, because he had no intention of bringing the letter into their intimate space—regardless of what the message was.

He would have eased into the oversized recliner beside her that they often shared, but he believed she needed some space to read and react to the paper he was about to hand her.

The expression on his face when he entered the den, where she sat, made her remain silent, her eyes fixed on his as he walked to her. He bent down, took her face in his hands and kissed her lightly—warmly, before straightening and taking the folded page from his shirt pocket.

She continued looking at his face. "What is that?"

After taking a seat on the edge of the love seat next to her chair, he answered, "Honey, the sheriff found this paper on Bender's body. This is obviously why he broke out of prison and tried to come here…to give this…to you. It's a message to you."

She widened her eyes at the paper in his hands, her mouth slightly opening in dismay and confusion.

"I've read it." He held it out to her. "I think you should read it."

Without hesitation, she took it, clicked on the floor lamp beside her chair and slowly read every line.

After a few minutes, she folded it and laid it on the lamp table beside her chair. She stared blankly into the space in front of her without emotion or change in her expression.

Finally, she looked at her husband with the slightest smile, taking him by surprise. "That's why he didn't die when Hank shot him. God wanted him to get saved. I'm glad he's in Heaven now. But I don't ever want to talk about him again."

She stood and reached out a hand to her man. "Come on, cowboy. Let's go to bed."

\*\*\*

# CHAPTER FIVE

Clint Berry headed out the door of the dude ranch bunkhouse just as Mitch was walking in.

"Hey Berry, where you going all dolled up in your Sunday school clothes?"

Clint stopped on the porch and gave his bunkmate a once-over. "By the looks of you, you're just coming back from Sunday school."

Mitch adjusted his fancy Stetson, pulling it down a little lower on his forehead. "Got a late date tonight, pard. What's *your* excuse for those spit shined lizards?" He nodded toward Clint's boots."

"Me? Oh…well, I'm headed over to tell a man I'm about to m**arry his little girl and** haul her off up state a few hundred miles to live…*And* take his grandson with me, too."

Mitch lost the silly smirk he'd greeted his buddy with and blinked a couple times. "Are you serious?"

He nodded. "As a two-year-old stud colt with an attitude."

"So…when's all this going to happen?"

"My brother called me last week. I'm needed on the ranch like asap. Dad's not able to help now. I knew this day would come." He cleared his throat. "There's a few thousand acres to see after."

"How does Abby feel about leaving home?"

"Oh, she's more excited than me. We want to get married—no fanfare—just say *I do* and head out. She insists she doesn't want a wedding. I gave my notice to Jesse."

"Guess you two are just going to quietly ride off into the sunset, then?"

"Pretty much."

Mitch reached out to shake hands and clasped his other hand on Clint's shoulder. "Congratulations, man. Your family will be in my prayers."

"Thanks, buddy." He walked off the porch, then turned his head back to look at Mitch. "Check SaraLou's water bowl for me. I forgot to look at it."

He chuckled. "You *did* remember to feed her, right?"

"Yeah, I think so. Not sure I could tell you my whole name right now."

He laughed out loud. "Hang in there. If worse comes to worse, I'll see you get a proper burial."

Clint laughed and gave him a thumbs up. "Right neighborly of ya." He got in his truck and drove out.

Mitch watched the back end of the vehicle leave until Sara Lou's sharp bark commanded his attention. He pushed the door open, expecting his furry sidekick to leap up on him, but she stood back just inside the doorway and began whimpering.

Inside, he squatted down, recognizing immediately that something wasn't right. "Come here, beautiful. What's wrong?"

She stepped between his knees and put her face against his shirt front.

"Are you sad because you're moving?" He knew that was absurd, but he talked to soothe her with his voice while he ran his hands over her, checking for anything out of the ordinary. When he ran a hand underneath her, she flinched and jumped back, turned and trotted into his bedroom.

It wasn't until he stood up and headed into the kitchen that he realized his left hand was sticky wet—the one he had rubbed down her underside. It wasn't blood. He smelled of his hand, then it hit him. Her teats were puffy. Milk?

"What the…?" He headed to his room and found her stretched out on top of one of his T-shirts. Apparently, she had pulled it off of his bed to make a nesting spot on the floor in the corner.

"SaraLou? What do you have in here?" He squatted down and ran his palm over her face and head. When she lifted her leg to check herself out, she revealed two tiny blue merle babies that were latched on having lunch. It was clear she wasn't finished birthing her kids and kept staring at Mitch and whimpering. She licked his hand, her eyes pleading for something from him.

"Okay, little mama…I'll stay with you. I'll be right here." He reached up and behind him for the pillows and sat on the floor with his back against the side of his bed. With legs stretched out in front of him, he relaxed, prepared for the long haul—and it usually did take a few hours. SaraLou calmed down until she suddenly began pushing out puppy number three.

Two hours later there were five tiny pups, all similar blue merle spotted, all females and all ferociously hungry.

He reassured the new mom, who seemed to have acquired a real attachment to him lately, then got up and headed for the kitchen. He delivered fresh water and food bowls back to her, dug out another T-shirt with his scent on it and changed her messy bedding, then left her and the newborns to rest.

He glanced at the clock and knew it was too late to try to see Daisy tonight—if she was even back yet. He also wanted to see Clint's face when he got home because he was pretty sure he wasn't expecting this. SaraLou had carried those pups without showing much belly. He'd had a little pony mare that gave birth one early morning without ever getting a belly on her. He grinned remembering his mama running in all excited to wake him up. It was New Year's morning and to an eleven-year-old boy, it felt like Santa had come again.

He found sandwich makings in the fridge, built himself a Jethro sized double decker and sat out on the porch to wait for Clint.

"What is it? Okay…"

Clint's grin spread the width of his face at Mitch's dumbstruck awakening when he tickled his ear with a twig.

He slapped at his ear, then realizing the problem, grabbed for Clint's arm to tussle him around until he realized there was someone else with him. He stood up from the rocker that had lulled him to sleep.

"Hey, Abby." He was groggily surprised at seeing her there so late. He glanced from Clint's silly grinning face to Abby. "What's going on? What time is it?"

"Ten o'clock and I'd like you to meet somebody before you turn in."

Mitch scanned the ground behind them. "Okay. Who?"

"My wife. I present to you Mrs. Clint Berry."

Mitch broke into an instant surprised open-mouth smile. "No kidding?" He stepped to Abby and wrapped an arm around her, squeezing her in a quick hug. He shook Clint's hand, pulling him into a back-slapping shoulder bump. "Congratulations, you two. How…I mean…how…?"

The happy couple both laughed aloud. "Actually, it just sorta happened," Abby offered. "After I convinced Mom and Dad that I *did not* want a wedding and Clint and I and baby Davy are leaving for Gillette soon to start our lives together—Clint said he told you that"—

"Yes, mam, he did."

"So, we just got Dad to marry us. We already had our license. We all cried happy tears and ate pizza and here we are."

Mitch chuckled at her simple sweetness. "Well, I gotta say, Mr. & Mrs. Berry, you are my kind of people. *And*… low and behold, I have a surprise for the happy couple. Follow me."

He led the way into his room where he had left a small bedside lamp on and waved a finger toward the corner of the room.

It took a few seconds before Clint or Abby saw more than SaraLou's blue, black and white fur stretched out. One tiny pup squirmed and squeaked—Abby gasped and slapped both hands over her mouth.

"Ohh…there's puppies!"

"Well, I'll be…" Clint exclaimed.

They both squatted down to pet SaraLou and fawn over the babies. "Would you look at this," Clint cut his eyes up at Mitch.

"I've been looking at this for the past several hours. Me and SaraLou are all tuckered out. There's five…all girls."

At the sound of Mitch's voice, SaraLou whimpered and focused her begging, tired eyes on his. He immediately responded and leaned down to smooth his hands over her face. "I know you're tired. You can go back to sleep. If a bear shows up here tonight, I'll kick his butt for you."

Abby giggled.

"Thank you for taking care of her," Clint offered when they got back to the front room. "I had no idea she was carrying pups."

"Me neither. She didn't show it. But I had a pony that did that when I was a kid…had a colt on the ground without anybody knowing it was going to happen." He turned to Abby. "So, what are the plans for you two?"

"Mom and Dad have Davy for tonight. This all happened so unexpectedly, we really don't have plans."

Clint looked down at the floor in thought. "It's kind of late now, but wonder if the Honeymoon Hideout cabin is vacant?"

"Probably is tonight, but I did overhear Ms. Martha telling Hank there was an older couple coming tomorrow. Fifty-year anniversary, I think. She was doing something special out there for them. So…are you off work tomorrow?"

"No. I'll be out by dawn. This wasn't planned…and I'm sure not complaining…" He grasped his new bride around the waist and pulled her against him, "but I won't leave the ranch shorthanded."

"Clint, we can just stay here tonight. I don't mind at all. I mean, you've got to get up early and I'll spend the day tomorrow packing some boxes."

Both men looked at her like a halo had just circled her head.

"And I'll take care of SaraLou and her babies."

Clint was suddenly uncomfortable—And Mitch was quick to read it.

"Well that's settled, then." Mitch turned and headed for his room. "I'll get my stuff and bunk in a vacant cabin…or something," he yelled back. "I was going over to check on Tuff anyway," he lied. On the way to the bathroom, he repented for the lie, grabbed his shaving kit, toothbrush, work clothes and boots and headed back to the front door.

"Thanks, man," Clint popped him on the shoulder.

Mitch affectionately pecked Abby on the cheek. "My girl in there might need fresh food when she decides to eat. A little diluted canned milk wouldn't hurt her."

"I'll take good care of her," she assured him, as he headed out to his truck.

Clint chuckled and shook his head. "You'd think SaraLou was *his* dog."

"If you ask me, she acts like she is."

He wrapped his arms around her and held her tight. "Lady, you're just full of surprises. I would never have thought you'd spend our first night together in this old bunkhouse."

"Clint Berry, you have a lot to learn about this country girl. I was practically raised in a barn. This bunkhouse suits me just fine as long as you're in it. I love you so much, my sweet cowboy."

She gave him a look that weakened his knees—but he managed to take a step back to reach the front door and lock it tight, before scooping her up in his arms and heading to his room—silently praising Ms. Martha for keeping the bunkhouse sheets and towels clean.


Mitch drove into the ranch yard and parked on the side of the barn. He didn't particularly need to check on Tuff, but he was beyond needing to know if Daisy was back.

Thankfully SaraLou had kept his mind occupied for the early evening hours, but now he felt almost desperate to see her and apologize for his rude disappearance those couple of days.

He walked to the back side of the dim-lighted stall barn and found Tuff lazily munching the remains of his hay. As he turned to leave, he saw something bright orange stuck on the side of the gelding's mouth. He unlatched the door, went in and pulled off a fresh piece of carrot from his mouth, that Tuff promptly snatched away from him with his flappy lips.

"Looks like you've had some company recently, old man."

It had to be Daisy. Then he noticed Tuff's mane and tail had been brushed to a silky shine. Bingo! His heart kicked up a gear knowing she was back and had even visited his horse. For some reason that pleased him the most—that she would spend this kind of time with his horse.

He left the barn and walked out into the moonlight. It appeared that all the cabins were still vacant except the one Daisy was in. Now that the escaped convict was no longer a threat, the dudes would be filling up the cabins and teepees—His work would be changing to leading trail rides, and hikes into the canyons, among other things. He'd always enjoyed interacting with the ranch guests, but right now nothing felt right except making things right with the cute little dudette in the cabin down at the end of the drive.

He glanced in that direction, unsure of what he should do—then, his heart bumped hard in his chest. She stood on the drive at the edge of the little cul de sac. He could see her form facing him in the dim moonlight—staring at him. He couldn't move for a few seconds—could barely breathe. Then he began slowly walking toward her until they were only a breath apart—face to face and silently speaking to each other through their eyes that were lit up brighter than the moon above them.

When she stepped into his space, they reached for each other and it was as if the whole earth shook under their feet. They held on to each other for a long time. This was more than an attraction of the opposite sex. It felt like a divine meeting of two souls, driven to each other—a moment where you know it was divinely appointed—when you know you just met the one who was made from your rib. Yep, old Adam didn't have a thing on him. Whether that was spiritually speaking or of his own natural bone—he didn't care.

He began to so gently run his hands down her back, down the soft material of the calf-length shift she was wearing. She tightened her hold around his middle and pressed the side of her face against his shirt front.

"Mitch." She whispered his name, wanting to say something, but couldn't think of words to fit what she was feeling.

"I know, baby." He pressed a large hand into her curly hair, holding her face against him. Neither of them seemed to be able to get close enough to the other.

He certainly hadn't expected this, but that fact made it all the sweeter.

She pulled back just enough to turn her face up to his. She wanted his kiss and when his lips came down on hers, there wasn't a person, dog or horse on the place—just her and Mitch. Nothing mattered—not her nightmares or painful memories or her life back home. She had no idea that there was a real thing called love—until this moment with this man.

He kissed her deeply. Her eager willingness was almost too much for him. He wanted to lower her melted limbs to the ground and to heck with consequences—but he wouldn't do that.

From inside himself, he managed to pull up the right versus the wrong of what he was doing—never mind what he was leading *her* into.

He grasped her upper arms and held her while he took a half step back, enough to break contact. He was breathing so hard; his heart was pounding in his ears. He lowered his head a moment to get a breath and when he looked back up, she was grinning at him.

"He had to chuckle. "So, you think this is funny, do you?"

"No, not funny. You just make me feel so happy." Tears burned her eyes from the joy that filled her.

He grabbed either side of her head and kissed her forehead. "You're killin me, woman."

"We should go to my cabin."

He groaned. "No, Daise, we can't." He glanced around, then grabbed her hand. "Come with me."

They walked to the pavilion and sat side by side on a picnic table. His long fingers closed over her hand and held it tight. "Daisy James, you better know right now that I would love to go to your cabin with you…for the night. But, my respect for you won't let me go there. And…I respect the Brandons too much. They have some hard, fast rules about that.

"I know. I'm…sorry. I shouldn't have…"

"There's nothing for you to be sorry about, sweet girl. I think we've had a mutual attraction to each other, to say the least. And I'm sure not sorry about that. Are you?"

She searched his beautiful eyes and shook her head back and forth slowly. "Not one little bit."

He leaned over and kissed her lips warmly, gently and quickly, then gazed down at his boots a moment. "There's another reason, too, Daisy…the most important one. Our Heavenly Father has rules, too and I highly respect Him…more than anyone."

"Are you a preacher?"

He smiled and shook his head. "Oh no, far from that. But…well…my mom spent years praying for Jesus to save my soul and He did just that. He kind of got all over me one day while I was in the pasture on my horse. It's a crazy sounding story, but the end result is that I have gotten to know the Lord. Mom taught me how to have a relationship with Him and I have a very high regard and love for Him." He shrugged and lifted his free hand, palm up, then dropped it back down. "I know that sounds a little fanatical to some…but…that's how I roll."

"Wow. No, that doesn't sound crazy. I think I'm just surprised at that level of…devotion to God. Especially when you're not a preacher or Bible teacher or something. I've just never known people that feel that way."

"Sometimes it's tough…like tonight when I'd like to go home with you and make sweet, insane love with you until the sun comes up."

She bumped her shoulder into him. "Knowing you want to be with me that way means everything."

Mitch laughed. "Oh baby, you have *no* idea how much I want to be with you."

He was realizing from her comments and the changing expressions on her face that she really had no idea how beautiful she was. She had changed clothes since he'd seen her on the patio ready to go into town. Her soft, buttery blonde curls begged for his fingers to get lost in them. And tonight, was the first time he'd seen her without heavy makeup. She was a natural beauty—fresh and soft looking. There was an innocence about her—and yet hidden were secrets that tormented her mind. She was quiet, not talkative—a gentle spirit. What happened to her? What horrible thing was she holding inside—trying to pretend it wasn't there?

Nonchalantly—although that's not how he felt—he brushed at nothing on the knee of his jeans and cut his eyes toward her. "Tell me about you, Daisy. Do you have a family—parents, siblings?"

She grew solemnly quiet while looking into the darkness. "There's not a lot to tell. My dad lives in Alaska. He left us several years ago and seems to want to be left alone. Mom lives out west of Fort Worth, Texas where I was raised with my brother and sister."

"Do your siblings still live at home?"

"No, they don't."

He knew he'd hit a touchy spot and decided to move away from that for now.

"How about you, Miss Daisy cakes?"

She fought to clear her thoughts that his questions had dredged up. She didn't want to think about her family now. She refused to go backward.

It took a minute, but then it registered, and she jerked her head around to face him. "Daisy cakes? Is that what you just said?" She couldn't hold back a grin.

He chuckled. "Yep, that one slipped out. You wouldn't want to hear what's rolling around in this head when I look at you."

Her grin widened. "Yes, I would."

"Okay, you asked for it, Buttercup. Doll Face. Sweet Tater. Madam Sexy…"

"Oh geez…stop!" She was laughing out loud now.

"I can't. You opened the spillway Miss Sugar Lips. Rose Petal. Sweet Tulip…"

She busted him in his gut with her arm, laughing harder. "Stop it."

"Oww." He yelped and bent over feigning injury. "Look what you did to me. I'm hurt. You know what this means, don't you?"

"Oh, let me guess. I'm duty bound now to marry you so I can take care of your wounded self til your dying day...or mine, whichever comes first." She shot a playful smirk at him but lost the smear of her lips when she saw him go suddenly serious.

"I was just thinking that. How'd you know?"

She laughed at his deep furrowed brow and inquiring expression. "You're such a nut case, Mitch. So, when are you going to get down on a knee and express your undying love and devotion and ask me properly? That's required before I can even think about it," she worked at a serious expression.

He glanced into the air in front of him, still stone-faced serious. "Oh well, allow me. I can sure fix you right up." He hopped down off the table, took her hand and pulled her down onto her feet. Then so dramatically, he stared into her eyes, that were glittering in amusement, dropped to one knee as he held her hand—never taking his eyes from hers.

"Miss Daisy Cakes, Buttercup, Sweet Tator..."

"Stop it," she giggled and tried to pull her hand out of his, but he tightened his grip.

"Okay, wait. I got carried away. Let me start over." He cleared his throat, twice, then took on such a serious earnestness, he was almost believable. "Daisy James, from the bottom of my whole heart, I love you. I've only known you for a few days, but that's enough to know that I want you for the rest of my life."

He let go of her hand and pulled a solid silver band from his finger, then took her hand again. This is my dad's wedding band. He gave it to me a few months before he died. Told me to wear it for the lady I intended to spend a lifetime with. It needs about nine pounds of tape around it to fit your finger—but will you marry me and wear this until I get your own—which will be tomorrow?"

By this time, her mouth was open, and her eyes were brimming. "Mitch..." She couldn't get above a whisper.

"That's a yes or no question... and I'm not laughing."

Before their meeting at the end of the drive earlier, her answer would have been different—hesitant, at least. But something blew through her when her eyes locked with his, before he even reached her, before they held each other those few minutes. *Something* had conveyed a message into the depth of her being that she would never be without Mitch Corry in her life. With him is where she belonged.

"She nodded her head up and down causing the tears to spill over the edge. "Yes."

He slipped the huge ring onto her finger and closed her hand to hold it on. When he stood up, she threw her arms around his neck and he swung her in circles.

"I love you, Mitch. I can't believe this is happening."

"Believe it, my lady. I've never been more sure of anything in my life." He pressed his lips on hers while he brought his arm up around her shoulders, pulled her heavily against him and deepened the kiss.

When he finally, reluctantly let her up for air, he knew this couldn't be a long engagement. He'd lose his mind trying to be patient for a wedding. *However,* she would call *that* shot. And he *would* be patient. *Help me Lord!*

"So, what do we do now?"

"I guess you could decide what you want for our wedding ceremony...like the date and who you want for attendants. You'll need to give your family time to digest all this. They don't know me from the goats in that pen over there."

Daisy took a deep breath, knowing she had no family to share her wonderful news with. Now is where she needed to be aboveboard with Mitch about her family—up to a point anyway. *And*—Lord help—her name. He has no idea that her name is not Daisy.

Mitch had already determined that someone in her past was the cause of her tormenting issues now and he could tell she was struggling with thoughts of it right now.

He stooped down to level his face with hers and smoothed his hand over her hair. "Here with me is where you belong, Daise...and you're safe with me." He watched her swallow hard to fight back tears. "I can take care of you."

"Its...not that, Mitch. I live alone and my life is...good. But...its only me. I am my family."

"You do have a mom, though, right? Where are your brother and sister?"

"They both died. My sister committed suicide when she was sixteen. She took some kind of sleeping pills my mom had in the medicine cabinet. My brother died a couple years after that.

That information came as a surprise to him and he felt genuine sympathy when he heard her voice crack. He moved her to sit back down on the table bench and sat beside her with fingers entwined in hers. "I'm truly sorry."

"Thank you."

"But...," she raised his hand and kissed his entwined fingers, "I have no desire myself to have a wedding. If you do, we'll plan for what you want. It's up to you. I have no family to tell or invite."

*Except a mother,* he thought, but let it go and gladly helped her lighten the mood.

"Daise...are you sure you don't want even a small ceremony. Baby, this is your special day we're talking about. Think about it."

"It's your day as much as mine. What do *you* want?"

When he hesitated, she shook his hand to make sure he was listening. "Mitch, I'm not going to make this decision alone. Tell me what you would like."

"Clint and Abby were married tonight by her dad...in the Luke's home. It was a spur of the minute thing. I mean, he went over there for supper and came back to the bunk house with a wife." He chuckled loudly. "I guess anything can go. They're moving up to Gillette to his family's ranch to work and live."

"Oh gosh. That's wild. So, he's the one who lives in the bunkhouse with you."

"Yes, and Abby is the daughter of our Cowboy Church pastor." He chuckled again and shook his head. "They just showed up a little bit ago at the cabin and said they were married. I think they were about as surprised as..." His words shut off abruptly when he glanced at her face.

Her hand covered her mouth and her eyes looked like she'd just heard a bad piece of news. She stood and backed up. "I…I'm so sorry. I have to go. Mitch…I'm sorry." She turned and headed toward her cabin at a brisk walk. How could she have let this happen? How did she forget? *Oh, Mitch. I'm so sorry.*

He didn't move from where he sat but watched her disappear into the darkness as he reached out and picked up the ring, he'd just given her from off the table. Stunned was a mild word for how he felt. Confused. Carefully he backtracked through their conversation but came up empty for a reason she would suddenly react like she did. He leaned forward, hands clasped with his elbows on his knees and stared at the concrete under his feet. What he knew he should do is bed down somewhere for the night and head out in the morning like usual—And let Miss Daisy James finish her vacation without him, then go back to her life in Texas. *That* is what he *should* do—like he attempted to do before. That could be the right thing—for his own peace of mind—or maybe he'd never be at peace again.

He put the ring back on his finger, then scrubbed his face with his hands. The wet drops on his cheeks shocked him. He couldn't remember the last time he'd cried, but it was a long time ago. He smeared his fingers across his eyes and swallowed a couple times. Why did he want this girl so bad? How could he love someone he doesn't really know anything about? Look at this ridiculous stunt she just pulled on him—talking marriage one minute and running away the next without explanation. Is this what life with her would be like? And hadn't he asked himself some of these same questions already?

He clenched his fists in frustration. "No! No." She was not going to run like this. He loved her. Whatever had connected them together so intently earlier was not something he could ignore. She had felt it too, just as strong. She would have to tell him to his face that she didn't love him and wanted him to leave her alone.

Determination brought him to his feet. He headed to his dually and grabbed a gift he'd bought her in town earlier—an unusual, beautiful leather turquois bag. It made him think of her when he'd spied it hanging in the leather goods shop. He had simply written on a blank tag tied to the strap—*For Daisy From Mitch.*

He walked deliberately slow to her cabin. He would not approach her—or any woman or child in anger. If his daddy had instilled anything in him, it was that. An angry man was scary to women and children, he'd said. Mitch never forgot that.

By the time he rounded the curve of the drive where he could see her cabin, he had calmed down. The porch light was off, but he could tell a lamp was on in the den. He didn't try to be quiet as his boots sounded heavily on the wood porch. He knocked loudly and waited.

"Mitch?" Her voice was soft and low.

"It's me, Daise."

The lock clicked and he removed his hat when she stood in the open doorway.

"We need to talk, Daisy. I can't wait til tomorrow."

She stepped back and he went in and closed the door behind himself. She looked so sad and vulnerable, it took effort to not reach out and wrap her up.

"Do you want to tell me what that was all about? What made you run off like that?"

"I'm sorry. That was a childish thing to do. I…just…"

"Just what, baby? You can talk to me. I'm here for you no matter what. But I need to know what is wrong."

He set his hat and the bag on the lamp table beside the door and stood still, watching her fight with herself about something—a thing he fully intended to know about.

Finally, she shook her head, continuing to look at the floor. "Oh god, Mitch. I'm so messed up. I can't marry you. I can't marry anybody."

\*\*\*

# CHAPTER SIX

The silence had become uncomfortable before he could break his frozen stare at her blank expression. It was the lack of emotion at her own declaration that had his senses arrested. But it was the reason he was able to keep his cool.

"I sure could use a cup of coffee. Mind if I make us some?"

She shook her head slightly and motioned a hand toward the kitchen.

He made the few steps there and waited until two cups had dripped before returning, finding her seated on one end of the leather love seat. He set her cup on the narrow coffee table in front of her and sat down beside her.

"I make a mean cup of brew. Don't let yours get cold."

She obediently reached for her cup and took a couple sips before setting it back down. "Thank you. It's good." Still emotionless.

He slurped a hot swallow and considered her for a minute. "What's your favorite thing in the whole world to do…your favorite pass-time?"

His question threw her off, but she was glad to just have a general conversation. "Hmm…well, ever since I was very young, I wanted to ride a horse."

The smile that broke across her face thrilled his heart.

"I don't know where that came from because I wasn't around horses growing up."

"Did you ever ride before coming here?"

"Oh, I had a friend in high school whose family owned horses and let me ride one, maybe five or six times."

"That's all the experience you have?"

She nodded.

"Dang, girl. If I'd known that, I would have tried to give you a couple lessons. But I didn't see that you were such a *duude.*"

He animated the word.

She cut her eyes at him and bumped his arm with the back of her hand. "That's a funny word…dude. Guess I sort of skipped the dude part, huh?"

"I'll say you did. You're what they call a natural. You sit a horse like you've rode quite a bit."

She looked back down, smiling shyly.

Hope had risen. They were conversing on a calm, even jovial level. He just had to be careful about upsetting her suddenly, yet he needed to get her to open up to him. *Lord, show me how to help her. She is so beautiful and doesn't know it.* He knew it, though and he wanted her to recognize her beauty and her worth. Security had been stolen from her by somebody. He might not know much about dealing with these things, but he *did* know that God had brought her here and was compelling him to help her—somehow.

His parents had been hard working and taught him their work ethics, but he had no memory of ever having been talked down to or abused in any form.

Pastor Judd had told him one day while they were hauling a load of grain back from town that there was one female out there somewhere that was made from his own rib—spiritually speaking, he was sure—and in due time, God would cause his path to cross with hers. The pastor was so right. He knew that as well as he knew he wouldn't rest until this angel—his rib—that was sitting beside him, was healed and whole and—his.

Daisy thought Mitch's interest in what she liked to do was sweet. She tried to recall just one person in her life who had ever asked what made her happy. No one. It sounded odd, yet so endearing. And she knew he was trying to smooth out the issue she had—the one that she couldn't visualize allowing another person to see and hear—to have to endure by marrying her.

But she loved Mitch Corry. He was certainly nice to look at—tall, wide muscled shoulders, slim middle—men who were chosen for sexy ads in magazines or T.V.—all *that* she considered a bonus. But it was the sweet heart of this man, the peacefulness and contentment with life that spoke through his eyes—And the look of pure love that he had lavished on her this very night, even from the first moment he had walked up to her on her first evening here.

She hadn't known this beautiful cowboy more than a week and the thought of leaving here and him behind shot a lonely, sinking feeling through her heart like she had never felt in her life. But she *had* to go. *Oh, God, I don't want to live lonely. I don't want to live without him,* she wailed inwardly.

"I have an idea." Mitch jerked her back from the emotional edge he saw forming on her face.

She sat up straighter, hope and confusion vying for a place in her head. "I'm all in for an idea about now."

"Good. How about I arrange a camping trip on the mountain? We'll talk to some of the others—Andy and Summer and whoever wants to have a little campfire adventure and pack up some saddlebags and ride out for overnight. What do you think?"

Mitch thought he had her up for a fun getaway when he watched her eyes light up with excitement, but that was short-lived. Just as quick as it shown on her face, she suppressed it and frowned.

She shook her head. "No, I can't."

Something told him not to push her. He'd had a little dog once who had been severely abused. She had strayed up to his family's ranch house and it took him a couple weeks to get her to let him pet her. Daisy reminded him of that pup—the kindest, most loving pet he'd ever had. He'd wished many times that the abusive owner would have come looking for her so he could have put some kind of hurt on them. Course, that was before his Jesus days. Even now, he wasn't sure what he'd do if he was confronted with Daisy's nemesis. But he *was* sure that she had some kind of abuse in her past. Someone had hurt her soul—deeply.

"Okay, well, that was just on my bucket list...taking Daisy-Mae James on an overnight horseback campout in the mountains."

The Daisy-Mae made her smile, then giggle.

Lord he loved the sound of that.

"You already have a bucket list?"

"Yeah, one can never be *too* prepared, ya know."

Daisy was trying to find the humor in the fact that a young cowboy would have a bucket list, especially *this* cowboy, but it wasn't funny. It almost scared her. She decided then and there that she'd never help him fulfill that list.

"Well then, how about I get us a big ole picnic lunch and we ride up the mountain for the day and picnic and be back before dark?" He wiggled his thick dark eyebrows up and down and grinned like a silly schoolboy.

She nodded in agreement. I'd love that."

"Done! I'll get it worked out and give you details soon as I get them." He gave her one quick pat on her knee as he stood to leave. If he stayed longer, chances were he might rock this gently floating boat. *And*—it was getting late. He stepped to the door, opened it and flipped the lock before he cast a glance back at her, then went out.

She stared at the closed door for several long seconds. The impact of the past few hours was slow in catching up to her, but when she glanced down at her half full coffee cup on the small, oblong pine table in front of her, it all came crashing in. Lying beside her cup was the ring—Mitch's dad's wedding band. She must have dropped it. Thank God he found it, but *no. This can't happen.*

She suddenly wanted to run out the door and not stop until she was back in Texas in her own secure little home—except that it wasn't secure from the awful harassment she desperately wanted free of. She looked toward the cabin door again and wanted to rush through it and into Mitch Corry's arms.

After a minute, she left the coffee cup and the ring on the table and went to bed. She knew her mind wasn't right. Making a simple decision seemed to always take an act of congress. Her emotions were immature—her thinking processes—according to the mental health counselor she'd been seeing. And she'd been working hard to become independent—To catch up with her age emotionally. But sometimes, like now, she didn't think she'd made any progress over the past three years. But she *was* living on her own and working—making her own way day to day. If she could just find a way to stop feeling as though every decision, she made was wrong—that every thought she had was stupid.

Then, there were times she felt as normal in her head as the next person her age—times she felt older than Noah's ark with all the wisdom of Solomon. What a perplexity of thoughts and emotions—up then down. No man could deal with her *stuff*—shouldn't have to. Never mind the persistent nightmares that brought her straight up and moaning—waking herself up night after night. And worse yet—*her. Her.*

She felt her belly clench as it prepared to cry—to strain deep down with the same gut-wrenching kind of heaviness that had come up out of her depths when she'd learned of her brother's death.

Grief had been a new emotion for her. She'd hated it but couldn't control it. This time, she fought against it. Why was she feeling this grief now? *No! Stop!*

She refused to let herself fall into this black hole of pain. Whatever it was that came for her—to torment her in her dreams seemed to be trying to get to her before she even slept.

She threw the light quilt off of her legs, got up and pulled her jeans back on—then socks and boots. Her pink and green plaid cotton nightshirt hung almost to her knees. She decided it would be fine for a quick walk around the ranch grounds. It was well after midnight and she was sure no one was awake here except her and maybe God.

She was so tired and felt herself sink in need of sleep but hadn't reached the point of giving in to it. She circled around the big horse barn and came up to the petting zoo pens. The little goats were bedded down and didn't seem concerned in the least at her presence. But when a solid something bumped the back of her leg, she squealed and jumped against the goat fence, bringing the small herd to their feet. They all began to congregate in the farthest corner, loudly bleating their concern.

It took her a few seconds after slapping a hand over her pounding heart to recognize Sunshine in the shadows. He whimpered at the goats and they instantly settled down.

Daisy squatted down and the sweet shepherd pup raced to her for a pat and rub. "Oh Sunshine, you took about five years off of me, boy. But I sure am glad to see you." She wrapped both arms around the furry neck and laid her cheek against his head. It was strange how comforting this felt. The pair had become good friends since Daisy's few days here. Sunshine always seemed to find her and ask for a hug, especially when she was alone.

He belonged to Andy and Summer Parker. Their home was a few acres away on the other side of the church building. Little Emma Jo had mentioned a couple days ago at supper that Sunshine always slept in the house on her bed so coyotes wouldn't call him out to play and then hurt him. So, what was he doing out here at the Brandon's place at way past midnight? If a wild dog hurt this boy, it would break her heart.

She knew the direction of the Parker's house. Maybe if she walked him that direction, he'd go on home. He must have a doggie-door where he can get back inside.

"Come on, Mr. Sunshine, let's get you headed home where it's safe." She stood and walked into the night, her furry friend beside her.

Laura Brandon stood up from her large easy chair in the den and stepped into the kitchen. A quick glance at the lighted clock on the stove told her she'd been up spending private time with Jesus for nearly two hours. This wasn't unusual, but the noise outside the house *was. Was there a disturbance around the goat's pen?*

Rather than turn on the outdoor lights, she reached for her flashlight, hoping to see whatever was there before scaring it off with the big lights. She unbolted the back door and quietly slipped out, glad to see the big doors at the far end of the patio beside the hot tub were open. Listening intently, she couldn't hear anything out of the ordinary. She waited for her eyes to adjust to the dim moonlight across the yard, then quickly pushed the slide forward on the flashlight when her eye caught unusual movement in the opposite direction of the barn and petting zoo pens.

"What in the world?" She whispered to herself when her flashlight caught a split second of someone walking out toward the church. "It's two o'clock in the morning." They were out of reach of her light within a second, but not before she thought she recognized Daisy James's blonde head disappear into the darkness.

She walked out a few steps toward the barn and shined the light back and forth across the grounds and animal pens, then returned to the patio and sat down at a table to wait. She had no idea what she was waiting *for*—but felt compelled to do so.

Daisy was glad when the pup suddenly left her and took off in the direction of his home. She turned around and walked back toward the yard, forgetting about Sunshine when anxiety hit her mind with force. With both hands, she raked her fingers through the sides of her hair, pulling it tightly away from her face. She felt like running—to where she didn't know. No matter where she was, the demons followed her and attacked mercilessly. "I'm so tired of fighting this," she said to whatever was lurking in the darkness. Exhaustion slumped her shoulders—a weariness that said she was giving up. There was no such thing as normal for her. Her beautiful-hearted brother and sister had resorted to drugs to stop their pain and she knew that was eventually responsible for stealing both of them from her—They lived lives of emotional torment that she only knew too well.

She had no answers, but she knew she couldn't—*would* not subject Mitch to this.

"Daisy?"

Even though the voice was low—almost a whisper—she jumped and sucked a fear-filled deep breath that became a squeal. Her hand covered her racing heart as she stared into the moonlit silhouette of Mrs. Brandon.

Laura put her hand quickly on Daisy's arm to steady her. "It's Laura Brandon, Daisy. I'm so sorry to scare you like that. Forgive me."

Daisy giggled nervously.

Laura chuckled. "I heard noises outside and came to look around. Are you all right?"

"Yes, mam, I couldn't sleep and came out for a walk. Sunshine was out here so I walked him toward home, hoping he'd go there. I think he did."

"Well that was sweet of you. Emma Jo and Rachel are crazy about that furry boy. I'll be sure to let them know you were looking out for him."

"I'm really sorry about waking you up."

"Oh no, I was up."

"Do you have trouble sleeping?"

"Well, not usually. I get up in the wee hours sometimes to pray. That way I'm not interrupted by…"

"By a dude who creates a ruckus taking a late-night stroll," Daisy finished Laura's sentence.

Laura laughed. "I have an idea. Why don't you join me for some decaf hot tea and girl talk? Lord knows I could use *that* with all the cowboy chatter I live with every day. Come on."

Without waiting for an answer, she turned and headed for the house. Daisy followed.

Inside, Laura directed her guest toward the small sitting room and busied herself with two mugs of tea she'd poured from a pitcher in the refrigerator. While they heated in the microwave, she took a moment to pray for right words to speak to Daisy James. She knew this early morning meeting was no accident. God set this up and she prayed for Him to have His way in this visit.

"Here you go." She set a tray on the large hassock with condiments for the tea, then handed Daisy a cup. "Be careful, it's hot. Help yourself to whatever you like in it."

"Thank you, Mrs. Brandon."

"Laura, please."

"Laura."

"So, despite the dramatic interruption we experienced this week, are you enjoying your vacation?"

"Absolutely. I've loved just being here—the cabin is so me. I guess I'll try and come back next year and experience teepee life."

"Oh...no, we are moving you into a teepee tomorrow. I'm just so sorry some of your activities were canceled. The dance band was booked up and we couldn't have our shindig during your stay—after having to cancel them because of the shutdown."

She lowered her eyes. It had only been a matter of minutes while walking outside that Daisy had decided to cut this trip short and go home—first thing this morning. She wasn't sure how to explain herself to Laura without sharing too much information about her and Mitch.

But Laura was on top of her sudden strained expression. "Daisy, is there a problem—something you want to talk about?"

She opened her mouth to say no, but at the same moment, a lump swelled her throat. Her eyes burned. "I'm so sorry. I just..." She set her tea mug down and picked up a folded paper towel from the tray to dab her eyes. She forced a slight chuckle. "I feel so silly. I'm fine. But..."

Laura waited quietly for her to finish and tell her what the *but* was.

"I need to cut my vacation short. I need to leave for home—this morning."

"I'm so sorry to hear that. Of course, we will give you a week anytime you can come back. You've paid for it, but...is there anything I can do to help you? Can I pray with you about anything?"

Laura's kindness was finally Daisy's undoing. Tears broke free and ran down her face.

"Oh, honey, I felt you needed a friend tonight. This is a safe place to talk. Only me and God ever knows what happens or is said in this room."

Being spoken to with such respect from an older woman who was about her mother's age—Daisy didn't know how to respond.

She was afraid if she said the wrong thing or showed an expression on her face that she didn't like—that gentleness would go away.

Just then, a vision flashed in front of Laura's face—a picture of herself kneeling in prayer in the empty cabin across the drive. The scene disappeared as fast as it had come. But she knew then that it was Daisy she had been burdened to intercede in prayer for that night. *Oh, Father,* she cried out in the silence of her mind, *show me how You want me to help this young girl.*

"I have nightmares, Laura," Daisy blurted suddenly. "Every night. Every time I sleep. I wake myself up screaming or moaning. I can't plan for a life outside of my daytime hours when I'm awake. I fight sleep at night until I have to give up. I'm so tired." Her hand spread across her chest and she lowered her face. She shook her head. "I'm so sorry. I didn't mean to…"

"No, honey, you did the right thing telling me this. In fact, I believe God led you here to our ranch. And this middle of the night visit was set up by Him as well."

Daisy swiped at an escaped tear on her cheek as she fixed her gaze on Laura. "Why? Why would God arrange something like this? It's almost a non-issue for Somebody like God. I…don't understand."

Laura studied her face. "Daisy, do you know Jesus as your Savior?"

"Yes, mam, I do. I got saved in a little Baptist church when I was about ten years old."

"Oh, that's wonderful." She clasped her hands together and pressed them against her chest. "I'm so glad to hear it." She paused to quiet her thoughts that were beginning to run over each other. She had so much she wanted to say to this child of God, but knew she had to be careful. Too much information, too quick, could do more harm than good. "Did your family attend church there?"

Daisy shook her head. "Just me. I walked a couple blocks to go. I wanted to be baptized and the pastor came to our house to talk to my parents about it, but my mom yelled and cursed at him and told him not to ever come to her door again. He never did and I didn't go much after that."

She nodded, a soft smile forming on her lips. "Do you want to talk about those nightmares? Are there people you know in the dreams?"

"Yes, sometimes there are faces I know and sometimes only a figure I don't recognize."

"Okay." She was thoughtful a moment. "Daisy, I'm asking about this because I believe our Lord wants to help you to get past it.

She stared blankly at her.

"I have a God-given gift of discerning dreams and such. He uses me to help people understand and get past problems like yours."

"So…are you like a psychic?"

Laura smiled. She knew to be careful of trying to say too much to Daisy. She was like a little child in her knowledge and understanding of God's ways. "No…not a psychic. I have no power to do or know anything. But when God wants to minister in some way to someone, He shows me, and I do whatever He tells me?"

"But…how does He tell you?"

"By the Holy Spirit who lives inside all believers. Sometimes I hear…sometimes I see something in a vision, or He might compel me very strongly to do or say a certain thing. It's always His choice of how He speaks. I simply listen for Him."

Her eyes grew in astonishment. "Oh wow, Laura!"

"Daisy, I'm not special. You have the same Spirit of God on the inside of you. It's a matter of choosing to learn the…well, the deeper ways of living for Him. Not always easy though."

"Has He shown you about me…my nightmares, I mean?"

"No, He hasn't. I believe it's your choice to say whatever you want to. He's not a gossiper, but He does want you to ask for His help. Then, He will gladly give it."

"I did ask for His help."

Both women sat in silence for a long minute.

Finally, Laura smiled and nodded. She moved to sit beside her on the small sofa and reached for her hand. "I'd like to pray for you, Daisy."

"I'd like that."

After a short and simple prayer for God to guide Daisy's steps into deliverance from her nightmares and replaced with the peace of God—Laura was surprised at the sudden declaration that came from Daisy almost before her prayer's Amen.

"I have to go home. I can't stay any longer."

It took a few long seconds before Laura could respond. "All right. You sound very sure of that."

"Yes, mam, I am. I'm so sorry, but…"

"We just asked the Lord for guidance, Daisy. Now we have to trust His leading. No need to feel sorry."

She nodded and wiped tears off of her cheeks with the paper towel.

"When do you want to leave?"

A wave of guilt swept through her. She didn't *want* to leave at all. She could barely stand the thought of leaving Mitch. And yet, there was an urgency inside her to go. She knew he wouldn't understand this and rather than go through the pain of him trying to dissuade her, she decided to leave before he found out.

"As soon as someone can take me to the airport. I'll catch the first flight out."

"Let me call and make you a reser…"

"No…thank you." Daisy shook her head back and forth. "I'll do that after I get there."

"Okay then. I'll have Jesse drive you as soon as he's up, which will be in about three hours."

"Thank you, Laura, for everything."

They stood and exchanged a warm hug. Daisy stepped back and stared at the floor between them for a moment. She *had* to tell her.

"Laura…I have an embarrassing confession I need to make."

"Alright."

Why was this lady so kind and accommodating? She'd never met anyone so un-manipulative. It made this transgression seem so much worse. She didn't know how to admit this other than to just say it.

"My name is not Daisy."

Her eyes widened slightly, but there didn't seem to be genuine surprise there.

"Thank you for telling me this—Are you Belle Ann?"

It was her turn for widened eyes and *her* surprise *was* genuine. "Yes…but…how did you know?"

"I guess I have a confession to make, too. A woman called our office looking for Belle Ann James. I told her we didn't have anyone here by that name, but she had a partial copy of your reservation form with our information on it and the correct dates. The part with your name was torn off of it."

Daisy's face turned pale and she sat back down to keep her legs from buckling. Anger was building inside her, mingling with the fear that had been rooted inside her for most of her life. "How did she get in my house?" Her voice was only a whisper spoken to herself. "She…oh my god…she was in my house!"

Laura sat back down beside her. "Who, Daisy?"

"My mother."

*My mother* came out with such venom, Laura waited for her to continue.

"When did she call?"

"Yesterday morning."

"Why didn't you tell me then?"

"I wasn't sure what to do because she sounded very…well…"

"Ugly? Hateful?"

Laura nodded. She was getting a clearer picture of Daisy James's nightmares. The woman she spoke with on the phone was worse than ugly or hateful—although not at first. She had a sugary sweetness in her tone when she first asked for Belle Ann, but when Laura was reluctant to give her any information because of the name difference—she became instantly rude and vile to the point of trying to bully her. "Do you want to call her from here?"

"No, but I do need to go home as soon as I can."

"All right. What should I call you now? I think you might always be *Daisy* around here."

"I like Daisy best."

"Then we'll just leave it at that. Why don't you head up to your cabin and gather your things—Rest a little while and I'll send Jesse to pick you up when it's time to go."

They stood again and shared a long, meaningful hug. No more words were spoken. Daisy went out the back door.

***

# CHAPTER SEVEN

Six hours after leaving the ranch, Daisy was in her own car in the airport vehicle storage lot and almost two hours later, she pulled into her driveway. She sat behind the wheel and scanned the front of her house. It all appeared as she'd left it, but she knew it wasn't. Her mother had been inside—rummaging through every drawer and closet and had taken no telling what.

Angrily, she slapped the steering wheel. "How dare her! Ahh!" She clenched her fists until her fingernails cut into her palms. She rubbed her hands together. "Well, this isn't helping anything."

She got out and found her door key in the flower bed beside the big river rock instead of under it where she'd left it. She could tell it had been thrown down in the dirt. *Wonder how long it took her to find it?*

She used the house key that was on her car key ring to unlock the door, but before she could turn the key in the latch, the heavy wooden door easily swung open.

Her heartbeat jumped into high gear as she reached around the door frame and flipped the light on before stepping inside. It was the middle of the afternoon and she was thankful for the sunlight streaming through the wide opened door. She went into each room turning on every light. Nothing seemed to be disturbed—except the extra copy of her High Point reservation was not in the small trash can beside her desk where she distinctly remembered dropping it. She had run a copy before she filled out her personal information online, which is why her mother didn't know she had registered a made-up name.

She placed both hands on the glass surface of her desk and lowered her head. Anger and fear batted around in her mind until despondency crept over her—She didn't want to do this anymore. Her mother fit all clinical descriptions of a narcissist and a psychopath and she could not seem to get herself free of her control. She'd been raised—more like caged up with her abuse until she finally turned eighteen years old and managed to land a job, buy a cheap, but decent car and finally rent a tiny, partially furnished garage apartment. For nearly two years, she worked and ate canned soup and tuna and slept—then repeated that process— fighting off her mother's constant visits to torment her. It was the laughter she hated the most—that evil, hateful laughter while she told her how stupid she was, how she'd never amount to anything, how she'd be fired from her job and —*you'll be calling me to come get you because you're on the street and starving.* Then that sick laughter would fill her ears. She could hear it now as she stood in the little hallway office alcove of her beautiful recently rented home surrounded by large oaks and two unusual transplanted pine trees. She had lived here only a couple of months before her mother discreetly followed her home from work to find where she'd disappeared to. The curses she had endured that day rang in her head now. *You can't afford this house. Who are you trying to impress? Have you got a man paying your way? You're whoring for this place, aren't you?*

Only when her tears splattered onto the glass desk and sprinkled onto her hands did she realize what she was doing— letting her mind be taken captive and into the past.

She stood up straight and turned a circle slowly taking in her present surroundings and situation, then spoke aloud the things a counselor had instructed her to do when this happened: "*I am in control of me—my life—my home—my job. I control my relationships—my friends—where I go—what I do. I alone control my life.*"

She did feel somewhat of a release after that, but why couldn't she get fully freed of this torture in her mind for good? And why couldn't her mom get a life and move on? Because she was emotionally and mentally sick—but, evilly smart—that's why! She needed someone to bully and control. That's how the counselor had described her parent after hearing the background of Daisy and her sibling's raising—according to Daisy.

Thinking about that description of her mother made her sad that she chose to live her life in such a dark, rude, self-absorbed place. The sadness was for her mother's wasted life, but she was angry and disillusioned—degraded by the one person who should love her the most—her mother—The one all the sweet greeting cards say always have your best interest at heart—the one she could always count on, go to for advice, a shopping trip, lunch.

"No!" Her hands covered her ears as if to stop her from hearing her own thoughts. Then she spread her fingers out in front of her and shook them as if to shake off the whole matter. It was her way of helping herself to switch her thought pattern—another step the counselor had taught her. It seemed to work, at least for a while.

Okay—time to get her bags and unpack—get back to her life. It shouldn't be hard to just settle in to the simple routine she had set up for herself. She had another week of vacation and was seriously considering saving it—going back to work. Too much time to think was not a good thing right now.

She had managed a short nap on the flight from Jackson to Dallas, but the all-nighter she'd finished off with Laura Brandon was taking its toll.

After unpacking and a quick hot shower, she fell into bed before sundown, barely aware that she did. The next thing she was aware of, the bright east sun was showing itself through a tiny opening near the top of her bedroom curtain. *Whew—what time is it!?* She rubbed her face up and down with both hands, feeling like she'd been hit by a truck. A *big* truck.

She hadn't quite decided to raise her body upright before her house phone rang. After the third ring, she reached for the extension on her bedside table without opening her eyes.

"Hello," she mumbled.

"Belle Ann?"

*Oh geez.* "Hi, Mom."

"You sound like you're asleep. I haven't been able to get you to answer for a couple days. Are you alright?"

"Yes...I'm fine. Just had a late night." At least her mom sounded like she was in one of her rare good moods.

"Your job said you were on vacation. I had no idea you were off work."

"Yeah...I was due a couple of weeks."

"So...are you just spending it all at home? Are you planning to go somewhere?"

Daisy knew her mom was baiting her—playing her *dumb* game to get her to talk. Well, this time she was going to let her know how much fun she'd had this past week. She was sick to death of walking on eggshells with this woman—fearing her wrath, her retribution for daring to think for herself.

"Actually, Mom, I've had the most wonderful week of my life on a dude ranch in Wyoming. I just flew home yesterday."

"Flew! Since when do *you* fly?" Sarcasm dripped through the phone line.

"I had the best time, Mom. I'm considering moving up there," she lied, but did manage to sound excited.

After a long moment of dead air—Daisy was surprised at the quick change of her mother's tone. "Oh...that sounds like a great trip. I'd really love to hear all about it."

Daisy knew she was lying about not knowing where she'd gone—And she'd never, ever wanted to hear any good thing that Daisy experienced in her entire life. But the sound of any degree of acceptance coming from her mom put a big crack in her defensive wall. Could she truly be attempting to change herself?

"I really would like to tell you about it."

"Good! My car is acting up so why don't you drive up here and I'll fix your favorite chicken spaghetti. You can tell me about your trip."

Bells were clanging—warning flags were flying in Daisy's insides, but she pushed it aside. "Okay, I will. I'll try to be there by noon."

"I'll be looking for you. Come on up."

Daisy hung up and with her hopes lifted, dressed and left for the two-hour drive, hoping to break loose the iceberg sitting between her and her mother.

A muscle twitched in his cheek as Mitch let Tuff slowly clop toward the barn after a long dusty day for both of them. The afternoon had been one of the hardest he'd ever experienced, mainly because he couldn't keep his mind on the business at hand.

Jesse had shown up just after lunch and told him he'd taken Daisy to catch a flight home. He didn't beat around the bush about it—just a quick *Got Daisy James to the airport.* When Mitch's face fell to pale, Jesse looked confused and added—*You knew that, right?* He'd nodded to keep from trying to talk past the shock that was constricting his throat.

Thankfully, Clint yelled at Jesse for something and allowed him to turn and head a few acres across the pasture to take some needed minutes to himself. He'd reined Tuff in under a shade tree and just sat there staring at nothing for several minutes feeling like his heart was tearing loose. *My God in Heaven—she's gone. How could she not at least think enough of me—of us—to say goodbye. A simple—goodbye.*

He felt the initial hurt changing to anger. Then a new thought formed. *Did something happen to her mom—an emergency that she had to leave so fast?* But that didn't compute. He was right here. She could have spared him ten minutes before she left.

He took off his Stetson and slapped it against his well-worn leather chaps. With his other hand, he raked fingers through his sweaty, flattened hair—then settled his hat back on his head. After a pat on Tuff's thin neck, he reined him back toward the busy side of the ranch with a resolve to get back to life before—her.

Now he was headed in for a dreaded, lonely evening. Having to keep moving all day—keep up a front, bantering back and forth with the hands while his heart was sitting hard as a rock on the bottom of his stomach felt like a slow, torturous death.

Clint and Abby were still staying in the bunkhouse for a few more days before they move to his family's ranch. He wasn't going to stay there and interrupt their first days of wedded bliss.

The cabins were now cleaned and prepared for guests that were coming in.

"Well, Tuff man, guess I'll be bunking with you for a night or two."

Tuff snorted loudly as if he'd understood.

"I'm going to take that as an agreeable retort. Anyway, we've had a few campouts in our day. We know how to make do, don't we?"

"Make do what?"

"Oh…hey, Pastor Judd." Mitch chuckled when he realized he had ridden to the doorway of the Luke's barn and no less than four pair of eyes and ears were rubbernecked his way.

He dismounted and dropped the reins on the ground before stepping into the barn alleyway out of earshot of the congregating cowhands. "Just thinking I might like to camp out for a change of routine. Was asking Tuff his opinion.," Mitch laughed.

Judd chuckled while he continued to untack his tired gelding. He was usually pretty good at discerning a person's emotions and this cowboy's laughter never reached past his vocal chords. Sounded to Judd more like he was needing some real alone time. "A campout can be real good for the soul sometimes. Unless you got a better spot for it, you're welcome to go hangout in my tent there on the back ninety. It's got a Coleman stove and lantern and a pen for your horse out back—cot and blankets. You've probably seen it up on the hill in the trees. The creek runs a few yards behind it. Help yourself."

Mitch was stunned. Sounded like just what he needed. He nodded. "Sounds good to me, Pastor Judd. Thanks."

"Anytime, Mitch, and I appreciate and understand your respect for my position in the church, but plain old *Judd* suits me."

He grinned, wishing he could resist better than this, but dern it, he'd blow up if he didn't say it. "Well, I'll try and remember that, plain old Judd, sir."

Judd bent and grabbed a brush off the floor that had escaped its bucket and pretended to throw it at him while he turned quickly, ducked and ran. "You better run, cowboy." Judd laughed.

The view was breathtaking. He knew as well as he was Mitch Corry that God, his Father, had led him to this very spot tonight.

He had loaded up and gone back to High Point for some of Hank's beef brisket and fixings. After grabbing some clothes and things from his stash in the barn, he made his work arrangements with Jesse and rode back to the Double OO with the crew. No one asked any questions. He just mounted up and headed for the back ninety.

With the little daylight that was left, he shook out the cot and couple of quilts, grabbed a five-gallon bucket he found beside the table holding the two-burner camp stove and headed up the trail for the creek to fill it for washing up and coffee. The pool he'd discovered in a section of the creek, a canopy of pines hovering over and around it, looked like the icing on this little oasis—until this!

The valley that spread into the night over the ledge in front of him was familiar in the sense that he'd chased calves and dragged them in for branding all across that wide-open space. But from this spot high upon a hill, sitting in a folding lawn chair, cup of smoking hot java in his hand and a million and one tiny silver lights twinkling over the valley was quite another thing. There was nothing to compare to the beauty and sense of Almighty God that engulfed his whole being. The orange glow that flickered behind him in the rocked-in fire pit, crackled and popped with the pine logs that he'd found beside the tent.

And, as hard as he'd tried to concentrate on this little piece of Heaven on earth, he didn't accomplish keeping her out of it. Daisy's image popped up in front of his inner sight and blocked out the real scene in front of him.

A fresh hit of anger and hurt rushed him and he remembered why he was needing a private place to be right now. He might get away from everyone else for a while but running to the far end of the earth wouldn't get him away from her. She'd taken up a prominent place inside him and he didn't know how to shut her out. Maybe he didn't want to. But—how could he survive his days hurting for her?

He stared out across the valley below him, then gazed upward at the stars dancing against the black velvet behind them. Even *that* had lost its soothing balm on his heart.

He slung the remainder of his coffee into the darkness, doused the fire and went to bed. Sleep was a long time coming.

Daisy was not comfortable with the idea of this visit and if anything—the uneasiness only increased when she drove through the gate and shut off the engine in front of the house. All the way down the driveway, she had scanned the fenced acre that her parents had worked long, hard hours on over the years—there was beautiful bordered flower beds that encircled every tree, a toppled-over old wheelbarrow filled with bright colored flowers until they overflowed and rooted into the ground—Perfectly trimmed trees, big rocks set in place with the tractor bucket and tall pots set inside a crevice between the rocks with a ground cover of flowering Purselene that spread over and around the whole display. They had called this arduous creation their showplace—and it had been beautiful.

But—that's not what she saw today. This place looked like it had been vacant for years. Scrawny, undesirable grasses had taken it all over and every piece of pottery or wood decoration was broken and weed covered.

When she looked back toward the house, her mother was standing in the driveway waving and smiling at her. This was definitely one of her better days, *thank You, Lord*. She had make-up on and her hair smooth and pinned up high on the back of her head. Her jeans looked fresh and new and a cute red, long-sleeve T-shirt bloused over the pants, hanging nearly to her knees. She looked the same as always—neat. The only difference was her big smile and wave aimed at her daughter.

Feeling better about being here, Daisy got out carrying her car keys and cell phone and approached her mom cautiously, not sure if she would accept a quick hug or push her away.

"How's my little girl?" Both arms came up around Daisy's shoulders and she reciprocated—still cautious.

"I'm doing great, Mom. I can smell your good cooking all the way out here."

She turned quickly and headed into the garage which led into the house through a laundry room. "Come on in." Her tone changed just as suddenly to short and crisp.

Daisy followed her inside feeling suddenly short winded—a heavy pressure on her chest. She knew it was old fears trying to swallow her and she stiffened up against it. Not this time. As long as this visit continued to be upbeat and friendly, she would see it through. And she had no reason to think it wouldn't be a good day.

The inside of the house was a stark contrast to the outside. Everything was clean and, in its place, just as it had always been—same furniture, same pictures on the wall, same everything since as far back as she could remember. There were no pictures of her or her brother or sister on display and never had been—or any other family member for that matter.

A metal bowl of dry dog food and a larger plastic bowl full of water sat side by side on the tile floor close to the utility room door.

"Sit down at the table and I'll bring our plates. I made tea."

"Tea is fine." Daisy didn't like tea and her mother knew that.

"Since when do you like tea?" Arlene sneered and smirked her lips.

*Just can't help yourself, can you, Mom?*

"I don't, but if that's what you made, I'll drink it."

Both were finally seated at the small round breakfast table and ate in silence the first couple minutes.

"This is good, Mom. Thanks for making my favorite chicken spaghetti."

"Well, I didn't make it special for you. You just came on a day I was making it anyway."

Daisy kept her eyes on her plate and swallowed hard trying to keep the last bite down. *Don't react. Let it go.* She took a sip of the strong, bitter tea.

"Well now, Belle Anne, I'm anxious to hear about your trip to that...*farm*... or whatever. What kind of vacation do you call *that*?"

Ugg—she hated the sound of her name coming out of her mother's mouth. It sounded ugly—like a curse word. She decided right then that she would find out how to legally become Daisy.

She sucked a deep breath and squared her shoulders. "It's a beautiful ranch up in Wyoming. A dude ranch. I stayed in a sweet little log cabin, ate supper every evening from a chuckwagon and rode horses every day. I've never enjoyed anything so much in my life."

She had no desire to tell her about Mitch, especially with the sneer that was glaring at her already.

"Did you meet a *sweet little* man up there, too," she spat.

Daisy met her stare for several seconds. Anger was fighting to take over. "You know what, Mom? It's obvious you don't really want to hear about my trip."

She continued to stare angrily at Arlene, not wanting to do this, but she couldn't hold it this time.

"Mom...you have despised me my whole life. You always had such a need to belittle me...to mock me over every step I've ever taken just trying to move forward with my life."

Arlene's eyes were flashing, one side of her mouth lifting in an attempt to appear to laugh. "Well you're the one who wanted to tell me about your trip. I'm just sitting here listening."

*Oh God help! This woman is so sick!*

"Now...so who runs that place? What else did you do there?" She heavily smeared that accusing tone at her.

Daisy couldn't do this anymore. She stood up and felt her stomach roil. "Oh...I'm going to be sick." She cupped her hand over her mouth and ran for the bathroom located through the den and down a hallway. Barely reaching the potty, she puked everything she'd eaten the past few hours.

Finally, weak as a kitten, she went back to the kitchen. She couldn't get out fast enough—just needed to get to her car and go.

Arlene was still sitting at the table, but where were her keys and cell phone. She glanced around on the floor, in the chair—nothing.

"Where are my keys and cell phone? I left them here beside my plate."

"You got so sick, I thought you'd want to lay down a while. I took them back to my bedroom and straightened the bed for you."

"No…I don't need to lay down." She headed for her mom's room at the end of the hall and quickly scanned the dresser, bed and side tables. They were nowhere to be seen.

"Mom," she yelled, "where did …oh," she turned and nearly fell right into her. "Where did you put them," she snapped? Daisy had had enough now and didn't care how angry she sounded.

"Well, let's see, honey. I got a nice quilt for you out of the closet there. Maybe I laid them in there."

Daisy rushed inside the dark walk-in closet, not thinking about the light switch being on the outside wall. When she turned back around, the heavy, solid-wood closet door slammed shut in her face—Then she heard the lock click.

*Oh God! Oh God!* She tried the door knob—Locked tight. "Mom! Open this door!" She pounded with both fists and screamed *Mom* until she knew Mom wasn't going to let her out. She heard another door slam and knew it was the bedroom door.

Her heart should be hammering in panic—Instead, she dropped her arms to her sides and stood still in the pitch-black closet, savoring a sudden gentle, unnatural calm that was oozing slowly from her head to her shoulders, middle and legs until it reached her feet. She let herself sink to the floor, refusing to lose focus of the easiness that had settled into her whole body, despite the frightening nightmare she was in.

After several minutes— "God? Jesus?…You're here with me, aren't You?" Her voice was the most minute whisper, fearing if she made a disturbance, the quietness in her soul would vanish.

"Please don't leave me." She wondered then if He had come because she would die here in this dark closet.

Immediately, Mitch came to mind—as large as life. A slide of pictures moved through her mind of his gorgeous face laughing, of her, enfolded in his strong, protective arms, of the two of them riding side by side holding and squeezing each other's hands. "Oh, Mitch," still whispering. "I'm not ready to die, Lord. Help me…live." Her plea went far beyond just getting out of this house. She was pleading for forgetfulness of all the traumatic events of her childhood, for the nightmares that had plagued most of her life, for joy and laughter and love. For Mitch Correy.

Sleepiness overwhelmed her then. She laid over and curled into a ball and slept.

Mitch spent the morning working harder than was necessary—he pulled several acres of a new four-wire barbed fence, insisting he didn't need help. Judd had eyed him with a knowing assessment, then reassigned a couple of the hands to another area who had come to help run fence— then left him to himself.

Tired was an understatement when he finished, but the afternoon proved to be even more exhausting. He had driven one of Judd's ranch trucks back to the dude ranch to tractor-pull a wagon load of hay riders around the countryside. Normally he would have enjoyed interacting with all the dudes, especially the twenty-questions-a-minute kids. But forcing a happy, chuckling face and tone was the hardest work he never wanted to do again.

After filling his belly at the chuckwagon that evening, he went back to the Double OO to feed Tuff who was stalled in the Luke's barn for a needed day of rest, then drove the truck back to his hide-out on the back ninety for a second night of wallowing in his jilted misery. Judd had loaned him the ranch truck to run between ranches—insisting he use it and not put wear and tear on his own vehicle since the driving was Double OO work related.

The Brandons and the Lukes were undoubtedly the most generous and kindhearted people he'd ever known. They always looked out for others whether employees or ranch guests. Or—for the man, woman or dog on the street in town who looked cold or hungry. His aim was to strive to be like them. But—right this minute, he felt like a failure all the way around.

He grabbed his bar of soap and a towel and headed for the cold pool in the creek he'd discovered the night before. His stomach was full, thanks to the Brandon's and Hank and Martha Walton and he worked solid for good pay and was provided a good roof over his head—thanks to the Lukes and Brandons. These people even looked after his soul. He was blessed beyond reason—and here he was in a blue funk, feeling like none of this was good enough anymore.

Beside the pool, he stripped down and stepped into the cold water. At first, it was a frigid relief—took his mind right off everything except getting his breath back after ducking his head and all under. It didn't take long to soap down from head to toe, rinse and climb out. That towel didn't do much for warmth and his clothes were filthy—so he took off trotting full speed up the trail carrying his shirt, pants and boots in the few minutes of daylight left. He sneezed loud enough to wake the dead as he streaked into the tent and hurriedly dressed. He built his campfire up to bonfire size wondering how mountain men used to manage in the snowy, frozen winter. When the answer hit him, he laughed out loud. He had just jumped into a freezing water hole in the creek, got out and run buck naked through the woods like no lean and mean mountain man would ever do—Nor would a half-sane cowboy riding for a well-stocked outfit like the Double OO. *Doesn't take a rocket scientist to figure out what that says about me, now does it?!*

He was still shaking as he lit the lantern and then the cook stove to boil a half pot of coffee. With a steaming mug in hand, he headed for as close as he could get to his bonfire.

He slurped a big swallow that was entirely too hot for any flesh mouth and immediately leaned over the arm of his lawn chair and opened his mouth to let it fall out on the ground. "Ahh—dern it! If I'm not freezing my rear off, I'm cookin' me."

He knew he had a bad case of it and he also knew he was going to have to make peace with this whole Daisy thing as soon as possible. Apparently, it wasn't God's leading that stirred his heart for her. Maybe it just felt good to be needed, because she certainly needed *somebody*. He didn't know what had happened in her life, but God knew, and he would pray for Him to send someone to help her—even if it wasn't in the Heavenly cards to be him.

That thought didn't make him feel better. The idea of someone else being with her and holding her, sent a pang of hurt straight through his heart.

The starry glitter twinkling over the earth tonight did nothing to soothe his wounded soul. Tonight, he didn't care that his eyes were burning with hot tears. He let them spill over and run onto two days of stubble.

*God, please. Help me out. I know You love this girl, but so do I.*

The next two days were long, but thankfully extra busy running between both ranches—helping out with the dudes and back to replacing old fence with new wire on dozens of acres for the Double OO. He did manage a hot shower in the bunkhouse before heading back to the tent.

On the third night, after Mitch's quick shower, Clint waited for him beside his Double OO ranch truck

"Hey, Clint. How's it going?"

"That's what I was going to ask you. Where have you been hiding out? I looked for you last night."

"I'm spending nights at the Double OO."

Clint looked away, eyes squinted in thought, then back at Mitch. "You squeeze into their bunkhouse? Last I heard, it was a lot too crowded in there."

He shook his head. "Naw…I'm camping on the back ninety in that tent Judd has set up out there. Got the comforts of home," he nodded toward the bunkhouse, "except for a shower. It's all good. Did you need something last night?"

"Just wanted to thank you for extending me and Abby a little privacy…but, I had no idea I'd rendered you homeless."

"Oh no. It was my choice to…spend some time by myself. Judd offered the tent. Like I said…I'm good."

Clint nodded, knowing there was more to this story, especially with Daisy James leaving, but he let it go. "I also wanted to tell you that we'll be heading out in two days. I'll tell you good-bye now in case I don't see you…And this cabin will be all yours."

They shook hands.

"Hate to see you go, but life moves on. Gotta move with it, I suppose."

"That's a fact," Clint agreed, reading between Mitch's lines, but knowing he couldn't say a word that would make him feel better.

"Take care of your family, cowboy, and I wish you all God's blessings."

"Same to you, friend."

Mitch got in the pickup and drove out. He was tired. It didn't take more than five minutes from the time he parked beside the tent to be curled on the cot inside the sleeping bag someone had left for him two nights ago. It was early, but already dark with clouds that blotted out the moon and stars. Fine with him. He pulled off his boots and scooted into the insulated bag. He was short on rest and that's all he could think about at the moment—blessed sleep!

When the truck horn blared just outside and bright headlights seemed to be aimed deliberately at the tent opening, he wanted to curse and fight about it. "Ahh people!" He bellowed, fighting to crawl back out of his warm nest. He was so sleepy, he felt drugged. "Just a couple hours," he mumbled. "That's all I need, for pete's sake!"

"Mitch Corry! It's Jesse. You awake."

*Jesse?* He shook his head, then rubbed a hand up and down his face to get woke up. Not bothering with his boots, he stepped outside the tent, a million things running through his head. *Did I leave a stall door unlatched? Water running?*

"Jesse?" He put a hand up to shield the truck headlights blinding him until he took a couple steps out of the glare. "What's wrong?"

"I had no idea you were staying out here. Clint told me where to find you."

"Is there a problem?"

"Well, maybe. A sheriff's deputy and investigator out of Jackson is needing to talk to you. Get your boots on. We'll talk on the way."

*What the...* He wheeled around and grabbed his boots from the tent, pulling them on as he hopped on one foot, then the other to the dually.

Jesse backed up and headed down the rough beaten trail. "Apparently a friend of Miss Daisy James's has reported her missing."

Every nerve and muscle in Mitch's body jerked. "What do you mean—missing?" He was boring a hole into the side of Jesse's face.

"I don't have the story yet, Mitch. They want to talk to all of us that had any conversations with her here. I only know that she missed an appointment of some kind and hasn't been heard from in about three days."

"Three days? Did something happen to her at the airport? Did she make it home?"

"Let's just wait and get the facts before we start borrowing trouble."

With a sense of urgency, both men entered the kitchen door of the ranchhouse. Mitch followed Jesse into the den where Laura had just served coffee.

Deputy Sidney Roston and Investigator Joseph Gann stood and introduced themselves, shook hands with Jesse and Mitch before sitting back down.

Investigator Gann got right to it—"Mr. Corry, are you acquainted with a young lady by the name of BelleAnne James?"

He squinted his eyes, confused and slightly relieved. "No, sir. I don't know a BelleAnne James."

The officer looked at Mitch in disbelief. "You have never met a BelleAnne James from Valley Edge, Texas?"

He shook his head and opened his mouth to answer.

104

"Mitch," Laura interrupted his reply. She hated to divulge information that was given to her in confidence, but she didn't see where she had a choice. "He's talking about Daisy. Her real name is BelleAnne."

"How do you know that?" Jesse turned a surprised look at his wife.

"She told me this in confidence, but under the circumstances I have to break that trust." All eyes in the room settled on her.

"So, Miss BelleAnne James, also known as Daisy James, spoke to you about personal things. Is that correct, Mrs. Brandon?"

"Yes, she was a guest here at the ranch for a week. She was out walking during the early morning, about 3am, and I was up at that time, too. I saw her and invited her in. We talked for a while and that's when she told me her real name wasn't Daisy."

"Is that unusual for you to invite a visitor in your house at that hour?"

"Yes and no. She was a guest on this ranch. I heard a noise outside. She was talking to Sunshine, my son's dog."

Jesse and Mitch were glued to Laura's face. Neither had heard this story.

"What has happened to Daisy? Is she alright?" Mitch was struggling to hold himself together.

"We don't know yet, Mr. Corry. We're trying to get some facts together for the Texas law enforcement working on this case. At this point, she's listed as missing."

"Missing since when?"

"That's what we're trying to determine. Mrs. Brandon, tell me everything you remember about her visit with you."

"Okay. She said she was needing to leave…to go home, even though she was supposed to stay another week. I prayed for her and then she told me Daisy was not her real name. I already suspected that because a woman had called our office just the day before…before our visit…asking if BelleAnne James was visiting here. We didn't have anyone registered by that name and when I refused to give the woman any information, she cursed and called me some really vile things. I told Daisy about the call and she was visibly shaken by it. She said the woman was her mother, but I never did get the woman's name."

"You said she told you she needed to go home *before* she knew about the call here from her mother?"

"Yes."

"Do you know why she needed to leave so abruptly?"

"She just said she needed to go right away." She glanced at Mitch. "I could tell she wasn't happy about leaving but didn't tell me why. Jesse drove her to the airport around seven that morning."

"I can tell you all that she *did* arrive home safely. After that we don't know yet."

"Oh…there is one other thing. She said her mother would have had to break into her home in order to have the information about her being here. She was very upset about that."

"Thank you, Mrs. Brandon. Mr. Corry, have you heard from Miss James since she left this ranch a few days ago?"

"No, I haven't."

"What is your relationship with her?"

Mitch stared at the officer, a myriad of emotions tearing through him. Finally— "We're friends. Nothing serious. Is there anything I can do to help find her?"

Officer Gann's eyes darkened as he stared hard at Mitch's face before finally standing, seemingly in a hurry.

"You folks mind if I use your lanolin? I need to make a call."

Jesse motioned for him to follow and led him to the office down the hall.

Mitch stood and spoke to the deputy who was slurping a last swallow of coffee. "If I'm done here, I'll be on my way."

"As far as I know, you can go. We know where to find you if we need more."

Mitch glanced at the wall clock over the stove in the kitchen. It was just after 5am, which told him he'd slept hours longer than he realized before Jesse woke him up. He also knew for a fact that his butt was headed for Texas on the first flight he could get.

"Laura, can you walk me out?"

"Sure, Mitch. Excuse me, Mr. Roston."

She followed him outside.

"Laura, I need Daisy's address in Texas. I'm headed there now with or without it. It would sure make it easier on me if I have it."

"Oh, Mitch, we have rules about this. Are you sure this is a good…?"

"I'm sure. Tell Jesse I'm sorry for leaving him short, but I *have* to go."

Laura decided if there was ever a good reason to break a rule, this was it. "It might take me a little bit to get to the information in the office."

"Call my cell phone as soon as you have it and anything else you can tell me. I'll be in range for a call as soon as I get near Jackson." He hurried off, forgetting that his pickup and Judd's ranch truck were both five miles away on the Double OO. It took him about ten minutes to throw a saddle on Tuff and head across country.

Thankfully the lights were on in the barn—Judd's dually parked beside the front entrance. Mitch dismounted and led his gelding down to the front of an empty stall to unsaddle.

"Hey there, Mitch Corry." Judd followed him to the end of the barn alley. "You just getting in or just heading out?" He patted Tuff's rump. It was clear he'd been rode a ways.

"Both, I think. Can you have one of the boys to feed my buddy here for me. I have an emergency and have to be gone for—a few days maybe."

"Sure. Is there anything I can do?"

Mitch led Tuff to the door of his stall where he eagerly stepped inside, then Mitch bolted the latch behind him.

"Yes, sir, there is. You can pray for Daisy James. She went missing after she got home a few days ago and I'm heading there now."

Judd's lids raised in shock. "I'm really sorry to hear that. I'll pray without ceasing and don't worry about Tuff. Where does she live?"

"Near Dallas, Texas."

"You be careful, cowboy."

"Thanks. I will." Mitch turned to leave, then wheeled back around. "Oh—your truck is parked by the tent."

"No problem. I'll get it."

The deputies were gone from the Brandon's when he drove through on his way to the bunkhouse. He needed to grab some fresh clothes and tell Clint what was going on. He'd never ask but hoped maybe he and Abby would put off leaving for a few more days. He hated leaving Jesse and Laura shorthanded this way, but he felt an urgency to get on a plane as soon as he could. Maybe it was just his own need to try and get to his girl before—before— *God, please let her be all right. Please.*

\*\*\*

# CHAPTER EIGHT

Arlene James stood at the end of her concrete driveway waiting for the sheriff patrol car to reach her. She had seen the vehicle come through her gate and rushed outside, purse and car keys in hand, thanking her good luck that she had dressed for town early—not that she intended to go anywhere. She just woke up feeling energetic and pretty. Her new mauvy shade of lipstick looked perfect today on her full lips, her foundation makeup smooth and dewy. She could turn the heads of men with her youthful fifty-five-year-old face—on worse dressed-up days than this.

With her sweetest pouty smile, eyes twinkling, she walked a couple steps toward the deputy as he exited his car and approached her.

"Good morning, officer. How are you this morning?"

He returned her smile. "Fine, thank you, mam. Looks like I just caught you leaving."

"Yes, you did. I was about to go out for breakfast and run a few errands. What can I help you with?" She could tell the man had noticed how pretty she was. His eyes twinkled at her. He was much younger than her, of course, but that was never a problem. Most men thought she was much younger.

"Are you Mrs. Arlene James?"

"Oh," she feigned embarrassment, "where are my manners?" She reached out a well-manicured hand. "Yes, I am."

He shook her hand. "Officer Stormer, mam. I'm trying to locate a Miss BelleAnne James. Are you related to her?"

"Why yes. She's my daughter. May I ask why you're looking for her?" Her eyes creased—Not with worry, but a burn of jealousy.

"Has she been to see you in the past few days?"

"Yes. She was here yesterday. I fixed a nice lunch and then she said she was going on a little trip with a friend. She's on vacation from her job. But why are you looking for her?" She repeated her inquiry.

"Apparently she didn't show up for a lunch date with a coworker a couple days ago. No one has seen her and can't raise her on her phone. She's tentatively a missing person."

"Oh goodness, she did tell me her phone battery was about to die and she needed to stop and buy a charger. She forgot to pack it for her trip. I'll call her continuously until I reach her and have her call and clear this up. I'm sure she's just fine."

The officer nodded in agreement. "Sounds like you are probably right. Be sure you tell her to call in." He pulled a card from his shirt pocket and handed it to her, then grinned and tipped his silver belly Stetson. "You have a good day, Mrs. James."

A shiver ran down her spine. "Thank you, I will," she cooed. Lord how she loved a man in a cowboy hat.

She watched him back out and leave, then got in her car. She was hungry. It was a good morning to go out for breakfast.

Trying to keep from having an all-out panic attack, Daisy tried to convince herself that if she died inside of this dark closet, she would at least finally find the peace that was so foreign to her life on this earth. She knew Jesus was real and alive and would take her into Heaven. She *knew* this and yet, there was still a fight inside of her to live—to stay in this life. It couldn't be her time to die. Or—maybe God had allowed her that last week of this life to experience her dream of spending days on horseback and experiencing the all-consuming heart pounding emotions of falling in love with a sweet, handsome cowboy—A man with big gorgeous eyes that had shined with love for her. If this *was* her end of life on earth, she knew she would take that one week into the glories of eternity with her and remember it forever.

She had no idea how long she'd been here in the dark— Days? Nights? It seemed like a long, long time. She had exhausted herself trying to kick the heavy, solid wood door in. Hunger had thankfully come and gone. But she was thirsty. *Don't think about it.*

Her gaze shot toward the door even though she couldn't see it in the pitch blackness, but she heard the distinct whining of a dog—then a scratching sound on the wood.

"Samson? Sam, my sweet boy, is that you?"

The whining increased.

The shepherd mix dog had strayed up here about seven years ago when Daisy was in high school. He had chosen Daisy as his main human, hanging with her every minute she was home. Her mom had refused to let her take him with her when she moved out and she hadn't seen him in three years.

His whimpering at the closet door brought hot tears. "Oh Samson...my buddy. You know I'm here, don't you?"

More whining.

She wasn't sure he was still alive until this minute, even though she had seen dog bowls of food and water when she came into the house. Daisy had named him Samson because of his muscular chest and shoulders. He had to be around fifteen years old by now.

She heard Arlene's voice for the first time since she had slammed and locked the closet door. "Sammy! Come out of here!"

"Mom! Mom! Unlock this door...please."

Samson whimpered again.

"I said come here!"

Again, a whimper—then a loud yelp.

After about five seconds, a door slammed.

Daisy knew her mother had kicked Samson or hit him with something. Apparently, he went out of the bedroom and then she slammed the door shut.

She felt weak with fear. She despised allowing Arlene James to cause her to break into a cowering mess like she'd done her whole life, but this time she was locked in a physical prison with no way out. She believed she'd gradually escaped the emotional cell Arlene had forced her into all of her growing up years. That had happened because she'd left home and stayed away from her for three years.

But she also knew what this woman was capable of— devious, hateful acts—but—*murder?* Would she really leave her in this closet, ignore her and let her die?

GPS was an invention of God, Himself—Mitch was positive of that as he turned his rental car around the last curve—according to the lady telling him every move to make to get to Daisy's address. *Your destination is on the left.*

He turned into the driveway of a remodeled older country home, white with pale yellow trim—manicured flower and shrubbery beds. A couple of huge pine trees were strategically placed in front and on the side of the house—obvious transplants. This wasn't pine tree country, but somehow, they looked like they belonged.

It didn't appear that she was here. He parked and got out, hurried up the porch steps and rang the doorbell. In ten seconds, he rang it again. After a third time, he went to the windows to try to see inside, but they were well covered. He circled the house to find the same situation—locked and closed up tight. The garage door was locked, which was exactly what he would have expected from Daisy.

He headed back to his car, deciding his next stop would be the police station. He needed to know where her mother lived.

Just as he began backing out of the driveway. A gray Toyota car turned in behind him and honked the horn. He threw it in park and jumped out, praying the outline of the woman driver in a short ponytail was Daisy. But a middle-aged woman stepped out and approached him with her hand extended.

"Hello. My goodness…word travels fast. I assume you're here about renting this home?"

He shook her hand. "No, mam. I'm Mitch Corry. I live out of state. Did you say this house is available for rent?" *Apparently, the little woman in his GPS was not on her game today.*

"Megan Writer, Mitch. Yes, it will be. My renter seems to have moved without notice and had a friend call me yesterday to tell me. I almost dread going in. These kinds of quick move-outs usually leave a major mess."

"Ms. Writer, was your renter a young lady named BelleAnne James?"

"That's right." She looked surprised. "So, are you here to visit her?"

"I'm looking for her. Do you know the name of her friend that called you?"

She gazed off for a few seconds. "Actually no, I didn't ask her name."

"Mam, BelleAnne James has been missing for a few days. The police are trying to locate her. I'm a close friend of hers from Wyoming. I flew down to try and help find her."

Her hand slowly went to her mouth while her eyes widened. "Oh no…I…I…then, who could have called me to say she moved?"

"You said it was a woman?"

"Yes, a very sweet, soft-spoken lady."

"Would you mind waiting here. I'm going to call the police. They need this information."

"Of course."

Mitch pulled his cell from his pocket but turned his back while he made the call and worked to get his emotions stabilized.

After he hung up, he realized Ms. Writer had unlocked the house and had stepped just in the doorway. In five seconds, he was behind her.

"An officer will be here shortly," he said more to the interior of the room than to her. She had flipped on the light to reveal a very clean, neatly furnished den. His gaze moved quickly into the dining area where an off-white, heavy, rustic wood table and chairs graced the center of a round rug the same color as the furniture.

The edges of the rug were streaked with Indian designs in red and turquoise. Why he noticed that, he didn't know, except that everything about Daisy was of interest to him. A whitewashed wooden sign hung between the two dining area windows with *Fresh Brewed Coffee Served Daily* written in red and yellow lettering. A large canvas painting of a white horse graced another wall. He could feel Daisy all over this house—sweet and warm.

Well this certainly doesn't look like she's even attempted to move out." Megan Writer voice was filled with concern.

Mitch headed down the hallway turning on lights and scanning each room before turning them back off.

When he reached her bedroom, his adrenaline was pumping. He wasn't sure the police would give him any information and he felt sure the information he wanted was written down in this house somewhere. He rummaged through her desk, then clicked the computer, but as he expected, it demanded a password to open.

"Address book—address book," he mumbled to himself as he searched her bedside table drawer. "Do people even keep address books like that anymore?"

Ms. Writer reached around him and stuck her hand in the drawer. She pulled out a small red book about the size of a playing card. She flipped it open to see the alphabetized pages.

"Here you go—address book."

The little book felt like solid gold in his hand. It was the first tangible possibility he'd seen of getting some information. He prayed Daisy would have recorded her parents addresses. He shoved it quickly into his shirt pocket when he heard the officer call out from the open front door.

"Thanks, Ms. Writer."

"I'll pray she's found safe for you, Mitch Corry."

After the officer took her information, he left in a hurry. And just as Mitch figured—he refused to give any information to either of them. He only wanted to know what, where, when, and how about the two of them.

Once Mitch left and reached the highway, he pulled off to the edge of the road and began with the first page, after searching the letter J. There was an address for Neil James in Alaska. He would start there if nothing else came up. And after that, start calling every number in the book. *Somebody* had to know *something!*

"There!" He jabbed a finger on a page in the middle of the book—under the letter M—Mom.

He grabbed his phone and set his GPS to the address. Hopefully he had the right mom. With his destination a little over two hours away, his adrenaline raced and popped. Sounded right. Daisy had mentioned that she lived a couple hours away from her mother.

He arrived at a gate of the address that he assumed was Mrs. James. From what Laura Brandon had told him, this woman was not someone to take lightly. If she had something to do with Daisy's disappearance, he was going to have to figure out how to communicate with her without raising her suspicion of him.

The gate was open—he drove in and parked in the circle drive in front of a beautiful older brick home, but the grounds were in need of help. Before he could form another thought, a woman came from the side of the house that was partially blocked off with a lattice wall and greenery of some sort weaving solidly through it. She came through a small opening in the privacy wall and hurried up a narrow path toward his car.

Out of habit, he reached into the back seat for his Stetson, settled it on his head and got out.

"I don't believe I know you, sir. My gate is not normally left open," she yelled toward him, stopping when she reached the front of his car.

"I don't mean to intrude. My name is Mitch Corry. I'm not sure I'm in the right place." He took a shot. "I'm looking for a Mrs. James."

A smile pulled on her lips as she took on a sensual come-on in her steady stare into his eyes. "I'm Arlene James."

She extended her hand and he removed his hat and held her hand for a few seconds. The squeeze she gave his fingers was unmistakable in her meaning. Everything inside him wanted to recoil, but a stronger force urged him to play along.

"Have we met…Mitch?"

"No mam.I don't believe I've had the pleasure."

She lowered her eyes a moment as if he was flirting with her and she was shy about it.

*Lord Jesus, I sure hope you're running this show.*

"I'm a friend of Da…BelleAnne's."

Something not quite readable flickered a split second through her face when he said *BelleAnne*.

"Oh…that's my sweet little daughter?" She glanced away quickly toward the entrance gate. "How nice to meet a friend of hers. Is she supposed to meet you here? Do the two of you work together?"

He forced a chuckle. "No, she's not and yes, we do" *We work together perfectly!* "Actually, I have some business up this way and thought she said she was coming here to visit her mom. She'd given me your address in case I had time to stop by on my way through." *Where are these words coming from?* He seemed to be winging it a lot better than he thought he could. Situations like this usually tongue-tied him. So far, he hadn't seen anything too off, except this woman's heavy flirting. No doubt, men found her attractive, even at her age, which he was guessing to be around 50ish. Her hair was curly like Daisy's and colored blonde. Her makeup was flawless, and she had a very slim build for her age. But—he wasn't one of those men.

"Well, it's just like her to have a real handsome cowboy for a friend. You missed her, though. She's already gone, but please come in for some coffee and a treat before you go." She jutted her lips in a sexy pout almost making him hurl.

*Hold your cookies, Mitch. You can fight her off and run if it comes to that.*

"Yes mam, I could sure use a cup of coffee."

"Well come on then." She moved to link one arm with his and patted his middle with the other. "And please put that hat back on. I just love a man in a cowboy hat."

*Oh God!* "Thank you, mam."

He replaced his hat and scanned the place as they walked down the path into a two-car garage. There was only one car there and he didn't know what Daisy drove. She finally released his arm when they entered the utility room of the house—spotless and decorated with painted open shelves that held clothes soap and fabric softeners and an old decorative sign that read *Laundry Soap-5 cents*. Food and water bowls were on a rubber mat against the wall. The kitchen was just as clean and shiny—nothing out of place or dusty. It almost made him think of a show house on a sales lot.

Daisy's housekeeping was similar to this, except there had been mail and newspapers and books stacked here and there, and her bed was unmade.

"You just make yourself at home, honey. Sit there at the table and I'll get our refreshments."

"Thank you, Ms. James." He pulled out a chair and sat after removing his hat and turning it upside down on another dining chair.

"Oh, let's just be Mitch and Arlene. Mrs. James sounds way too old for me. And besides that, I *don't* have a husband now."

He nodded slightly—pulled his lips in an almost smile and darted his eyes toward the large den adjacent to the kitchen. Then he froze! His heart instantly began to hammer on the bones of his rib cage, and he swallowed hard. No way was there another one like that!

The one-of-a-kind turquoise soft leather shoulder bag that he had bought Daisy when he and Jesse had gone to Jackson Hole for feed one day, was sitting on a little side table inside the den. There was no mistaking it. It was hand-stitched by Lillie Dogwood with a muted Indian red and turquoise fringe combination that gave it it's one and only signature statement. Every purse Lillie ever made was different. This one was eye-popping sitting among the others in her leather goods shop. *Why is it sitting on that table? This woman is not right—not normal in her head. Has she done something to harm Daisy?* Then the dog bowls crossed his mind.

"I noticed you have food and water out for a dog? What kind do you have? I really love dogs." He smiled, thinking he was going to choke with this small talk crap, but he couldn't blow this. He was talking to a mentally disturbed woman.

"Oh, just a mutt. He's been a very bad boy today so he's in his outside house."

He forced a laugh. "Guess he better learn to behave."

Arlene set a full cup of black coffee and a spoon in front of him. She retrieved a small bowl from inside a cabinet containing packets of sugar and coffee creamer, then set a package of brownies on the table between them and took her seat.

"These little cakes are delicious. I keep them on hand for special company. Please have one."

He took one from the package and took a bite and a sip of the strong black coffee. He wanted to spit it all out. He'd play-acted about as long as he could stand. His stomach had knotted at the sight of Daisy's purse. She could have left here without it if she was in that big of a hurry and if her car keys were not in it.

As he was about to jump up and head into the next room to examine the purse, an even stronger force held him in his chair. He knew instantly that God Almighty's Hand was on him. He calmed himself and remained seated, but Arlene had noticed his uneasiness.

"Is something wrong, Mitch? She cooed.

He swallowed another sip of coffee to stall for time. "No mam. I just noticed that eye-catching purse sitting on the table in there." He nodded toward the big living room. "I've never seen anything that pretty."

She turned her whole body around and leaned forward to see what he was referring to. "Oh my, I've had that old thing for a long time. I meant to put it away after...I went through some old pictures I had stored in it."

"It's pretty, just like your home. I admire a lady who takes such good care of her home."

"Thank you. I would offer you a tour, but...well...the other end of my home is rather personal. I don't keep it quite as neat as this part." She stood and gathered the cups and cakes and headed toward the sink—obviously agitated.

Mitch stood and picked up his hat. Something was wrong in this house and he intended to find out what.

"Arlene, thank you for your hospitality. I enjoyed meeting you, but I've got to get on down the road."

She turned around sporting a sweet smile that went no further than her lips. Those eyes were angry.

"I have an errand to run myself, but you come again anytime." She walked him outside and watched until he drove out of the gate.

Likewise, he watched her through his rearview until he turned onto the highway and drove a couple miles. She was in a hurry for him to leave and he was going to find out why. Everything about her demeanor changed when he mentioned that purse—Daisy's purse.

He turned onto a narrow dirt road, more like an off-road jeep trail. It made a sharp curve just a few yards in—He parked, locked up and started walking through a densely wooded area. He hadn't noticed any houses along the highway on this side. He would find a spot and wait for a chance to look through Arlene's house. If she was the one who had called Daisy's landlady yesterday, maybe he could check numbers on the house phone that he'd seen lighted on her kitchen counter.

After nearly an hour of crossing barbed-wire fences and forging a trail through mostly woods and a short run across an open field of knee-high grasses—he spotted her barn that was about three acres away from her back door.

Her car was still parked in the same place on her driveway. He had hoped that she did have an errand to run and would leave.

A few yards from the barn, he spotted Arlene in front of her car talking on a cell phone. He hid behind a large oak tree trying to hear her words, but he could only make out her boisterous laughter every now and then.

Squatted down on one knee, he waited. If he didn't get a chance to get inside the house, he'd get to the barn and wait it out.

As luck would have it—Arlene appeared to have ended her call, quickly got in her car and backed out. Instead of heading toward her front gate, she drove up to the front of the barn. When she got out and went inside, Mitch froze, his eyes wide when he saw Daisy's purse in her hand. She came back out within thirty seconds—minus the purse.

"What the…" He swallowed hard, barely able to stay still.

She drove out then and as soon as her car disappeared from his view, he ran all the way to the barn. He shoved open the small side door that Arlene had used and after one step inside, he stopped dead in his tracks.

A white Honda Civic set in the center of the barn. Somehow, he knew this was Daisy's vehicle. He rushed to pull open the driver's door and there set the leather turquoise purse. He grabbed it out and dumped it on the narrow ledge of concrete behind the car. A ring of keys pinged on the floor, an envelope that he grabbed up and saw it was addressed to Mrs. Megan Writer—Daisy's landlady. It had a stamp on it for mailing but had been ripped open. He pulled out a statement showing the amount due, but there was no money inside. The statement, however, had Mrs. Writer's address and—a phone number.

Realizing what this information meant, he left everything where it was, urgently scanning the interior of the barn. His teeth hurt from gritting them so hard and his brain felt like it could pop wide open with every horrible thought cutting trenches through his head.

"Daisy!" He yelled

Then he reached into the open car door and pushed the trunk release. It popped open, but it was spotless and empty. Without closing the trunk or front car door, he raced outside not looking nor caring if Arlene had returned.

He stood still long enough to punch in a 911 call and ask for help from the sheriff's department. "Send an ambulance. She's out here somewhere. Hurry up."

"Sir, I need you to calm down and I need you to stay on the phone."

"I can't stay on the phone. I have to get in that house. Just get me some help." He broke the connection and ran to the garage.

The entrance door was locked. He headed around the house trying every door and window, with no luck.

Sprinting around a deck that jutted out several feet in the back yard, he startled the *mutt* who had been a *bad boy.* The dog barked and growled at Mitch, the hair on his neck standing straight up. The pen he was in was barely big enough for him to walk around. There was no overhead shelter, food or water in there. Just a fully enclosed wire cage.

Mitch approached the cage slowly. "Hey, buddy. Somebody's being bad and I don't believe for a second it's you." He stuck a hand against the wire so the dog could smell. Then he began to whine and wag his tail, begging with large, round, sad eyes— Mitch stuck his fingers inside for a gentle touch. Then he unsnapped the latch and opened the door.

The whining and butt wiggling sent Mitch to his knee so he could return the hugs and make fast friends for about twenty seconds.

"Okay, boy, let's get inside. Your water and food is in there."

Without another thought or give-a-rip—he picked up a metal lawn chair from the deck and crashed a nice sized hole in a den window. Carefully he stepped through, then unlocked it and opened it for the dog.

"Go get you some water, my man."

The dog took off at a stretched-out sprint, but not toward his water. He went the other way down a long hallway. Mitch followed at a sprint of his own. The dog was frantically scratching and whining at a closed door at the very end of the hall. He grasped the door knob and opened it.

In a glance, the bedroom was neat and as clean as the kitchen was. In the next heartbeat, he was beside a frantic dog at the closed closet door. It was locked, but the heavy-duty bolt turned easily, and he pulled the door open.

"Sweet Jesus! God…no! Daisy…baby? Daisy?"

A urine odor filled the closet space, infuriating him more at the sick woman who had locked her in here.

She was curled in a fetal position, face turned into the carpeted floor. Gently he slid a hand beneath her shoulders and turned her over to see her face. She was unconscious, but a pulse was there.

The dog tried to get on top of her, to lick her face, but Mitch pushed him back. "No, dog. Sit" Samson obediently sat but frowned and whimpered while staring at his favorite human.

Mitch grasped her under the arms and pulled her limp body until her head was out in the fresher air. As he was reaching for his cell to call 911 again—his blood chilled at the sound behind him.

"You! How dare you come in my house when I'm gone!"

He left the cell in his pocket and wheeled around. His first instinct was to rush her and restrain her until law enforcement arrived—but the barrel of a 357 Magnum in his face changed that impulse.

"Arlene, your daughter needs help. She's unconscious."

The curled-lip sneer on her face literally made him feel nauseated. It was like looking into the face of the devil.

"My *daughter,* huh." Her voice was low and guttural. "I don't have a *daughter,*" she spat.

He had to keep her talking and pray for help to get here—fast.

"Arlene, you're not feeling well, are you? That's all this is. You are just not thinking clearly. We need to get you checked out—maybe get you some medicine."

He watched her face change a little—the brittleness in her eyes softened.

"BelleAnne must have gotten accidentally locked in this closet. She's not well and she's going to need you to take care of her while she recovers. Do you think she can stay here with you for a few days?" He had no idea what he was even saying. Words just kept pouring out of his mouth.

Confusion took over her countenance now.

"I'm so glad you came home. I heard noises in here and thought *you* might have needed help. Then I found *her.* She needs your help, Arlene."

She seemed to have forgotten the gun. It was pointing at the floor in her limp hand. This would have been the moment to rush her before she switched personalities or whatever was happening to her—except a sheriff's deputy was standing behind her, an arm's reach from her.

"Everything will be all right now, Arlene."

The deputy grabbed her upper arm and the gun at the same time. She screamed in fear, then peppered him with a string of obscenities. More officers entered the room, one of them radioed for EMS outside to come in.

Once Daisy was lifted into the ambulance, an IV was started for severe dehydration and she was given a solution of sugar. Her blood sugar level was low, causing her to pass out. She woke up almost immediately and when she saw Mitch's face, she began to weep, reaching for him. They allowed him to hold her until she calmed down.

"Where's my mother?"

"They're taking her where she can eventually get some help, Daise."

"Sam. Will you take Sam with you."

"Sam?"

When she spoke his name, the dog tried to leap into the open ambulance.

"Ah, so that's your name. Sam. Don't worry about him. We're best buds now. I'll take care of him."

"Thank you, Mitch." She began to cry again.

"I'll see you in a little while." He stepped back and let the medic's close the doors.

He knew he'd be a while giving his account of things to the sheriff, but before he spoke a word to them, he gave thanks and praise to his Heavenly Father.

\*\*\*

# CHAPTER NINE

Mitch rapped on the partially opened door of Daisy's hospital room before he pushed it wider and stuck his head in. An I.V. drip was going in her arm. Her face was turned away from him and she appeared to be asleep.

He went in and walked around the bed so he could see her face—She wasn't asleep, and his heart sank at the pain and torment in her eyes. She was staring at the wall then slowly cut her eyes toward him. *My God, what had that monster done to her?*

"The police were here." Her voice was soft, but monotoned. "They said you were the one who found me. Thank you."

He stepped to the edge of the bed and she averted her eyes, looking at the floor. When he covered her hand with his, she pulled free and curled a fist against her chest. He wanted to pull her up into his arms so bad and hold her until she knew she was safe with him.

"Daisy, the thanks should go to Samson. He led me straight to you. I didn't have to search hard. He's your hero."

She started to glance up at him like she had something to say, then pulled back into her shell.

"They told me you could be released to go home tomorrow. I'll be staying at the Carrikker House tonight. It's a motel that let me keep Sam in my room."

She didn't so much as blink—still staring at the floor.

"I have your car. Your purse is locked in the trunk. I'll bring it up here if you need it."

She nodded her head. "I do. Thanks," she whispered.

He didn't go into any other details or try to ask questions. She was clearly traumatized and just needed time to process this nightmare she experienced the past four days. He intended to give her all the time she needed, and he would be there for her as long as it took.

"I'll be right back with your bag. Can I get you anything else? Something to drink?"

She shook her head and he patted her foot through the blanket as he passed the end of her bed on his way out.

Within fifteen minutes, he was back. She hadn't moved a muscle and still wouldn't look at him. As bad as it hurt his heart, he refused to believe she meant any of this toward him. He couldn't ignore the fact that she had left the ranch without a word of goodbye to him, but she would have to tell him to his face to leave her—that she didn't love him. He knew full well what he'd seen in her eyes that night on the drive-in front of the barn at the ranch. They both felt something close to an electric current waving between them when they touched—kissed—held each other under the night sky. No! There was something else—something he had to find out about.

"Daise, your bag is in the drawer of this table." He wanted to wrap his arms around her. He wanted to slide into her bed and hold her while she slept. "I left my cell number at the nurse's desk and I wrote it down for you and put it in your purse."

No response.

"I love you, Daisy. Good night." He left.

*I love you, Mitch Corry.* Her pent-up emotions broke loose when she heard the door close. She couldn't face him—ever. Not now. Her free hand covered her face as she dissolved in tears.

Dressed in the only extra clothes he brought, the black sweat pants were a little heavy for Texas in September, but his extra-large white T was loose and cool. He stretched out on the padded chaise lounge on the small balcony attached to his third story room and watched Sam sleeping peacefully against the balcony railing. They had picnicked outside the car in the parking area—Sam pottied and here they were bunking together like longtime roommates. The one thing they did have in indisputable common was they both loved the same woman.

"I'm glad you're a dog, Sam. I can compete with that."

Samson raised his head and whimpered at Mitch as though he understood.

"Yeah, I know. She's going to need all of both of us. We better just stick together and get her through this."

*And then what?*

He released a weary sigh. Truth was, she didn't want comfort from him. She didn't even want him in her room.

The image of her small body curled up in the floor of that closet came into his mind—a vision that seemed to come against his will. He didn't want to remember that scene. He wasn't sure at first sight that she was alive. When he felt a pulse beat in her wrist—her breath on his face—it was as if his heart had stopped, then roared back to life. That beautiful, young cowgirl had a grip on his soul that was a forever deal. It was like they were connected much deeper than just a simple attraction. If he had to leave and go home without her—his life would be forever altered and not for the better. Just the thought was painful.

Running both hands over his eyes and down his face, he gazed out at the lightning flashes against the far horizon. He used to love storms. But tonight, it only reminded him of the hurtful situation Daisy had just endured. What happens to the brain of people like Arlene James? He couldn't relate to that kind of treatment and feelings in any circumstance—but a mother using such evil actions against her own daughter? That didn't make sense in his head.

At least the law enforcement officers were more than kind and helpful to him. After giving the investigators a lengthy statement and showing them the car and purse in the barn—they drove him back to his rental car he'd left on the dirt road and followed him in to a rental agency to turn it in, then back to Arlene's to get Daisy's car and Samson.

He'd locked up the house after covering the broken window with a heavy piece of plywood he found in the garage, along with hammer and nails in a shop cabinet.

Arlene's house and car keys were placed into Daisy's purse where she could find them. He had no idea what would become of Mrs. James, but he didn't figure she'd be back home for a long time—if ever.

And—thinking of home—he reached into his pocket for his cell to give Jesse and Laura a call and let them know what had happened down here.

Daisy opened her eyes. It took a few seconds to remember where she was—then it all came flooding back.

Lightening slashed a yellow streak through the partially open window blinds. Otherwise she awoke in black darkness—which suited her just fine. There seemed to be a comfort of some kind laying there with the storm outside, shaking with anger because it couldn't reach her. It was almost like a sign that said—she can't reach you now. You're safe. Even in the darkness—you're safe.

The peace she felt oozing through her entire being was indescribable. No fear—no cares—just sweet Holy peace.

"Yes," she whispered, "Holy. Thank You, my God in Heaven. Thank You. Thank You."

Sweet sleep took her then.

"Miss James, can you wake up and eat some breakfast while it's hot?"

Daisy peeked out of sleepy eyes to see a bright sun looking back at her through the same blind she'd just watched lightening spark through. That seemed like five minutes ago.

She turned onto her back, mindful of the IV tubes attached to her hand.

"Morning, glory!" The nurse smiled broadly at her while she took her vitals. "Can I help you up to the bathroom before I go?"

"Thank you. I can probably get there, myself."

"Well, I'll push this bottle of joy juice for you anyway. It's about empty and I don't think you have any more ordered."

Daisy grabbed the purse Mitch had brought the evening before, the one he had bought her in Jackson Hole and surprised her with. She would treasure it forever—not because it was a handmade, one of a kind, but because Mitch Corry gave it to her.

Once inside the tiny bathroom, she sent the nurse on her way and dug out her make-up bag. After doing a quick fix-up on her hair and face, she pushed the IV pole out and settled on the side of the bed where she could get at the bacon and coffee she smelled. She was starved, but before she got to the food—it hit her—If Mitch had her car with her keys, what was jingling down in her purse just now.

She reached for the bag on the foot of her bed and dug deep inside, pulling out an unfamiliar set of keys.

There were four keys on a large stainless-steel ring—and a small locket attached to another smaller ring. Opening the locket, she caught her breath at the two pictures inside. A youthful picture of her mother holding a little toddler boy—her brother—and a single picture of her brother as a teenager on the opposite side. It didn't surprise her at all that neither her picture nor her sisters were there. These were her mom's keys to her house and her car. Why were these in *her* purse?

She let herself recall the details from—was it just yesterday? Her mom was arrested. She had meant to let her die in that closet. Mitch came.

She was suddenly mortified at the remembrance—the closet. Mitch had found her. *Oh no.* She couldn't bear to remember. The thought made her recoil—her heart feeling like it was chipped with sharp edges cutting her insides.

With that thought, she looked up to see Mitch Corry carrying a pretty blue-flowery plastic bag and standing in the open doorway. Beside him stood— "Sam!"

On instant recognition of her voice, the dog pulled away from Mitch's loose hold on his leash and bounded on top of the bed in one leap. Oddly Mitch's first thought was how glad he was that he had bathed and foo-fooed Sam up this morning.

Daisy squealed in delight as he wiggled and licked her face, while Mitch covered the few steps to get a grip on his collar. But—not before a plate of scrambled eggs and bacon flew off the table that had been rolled up beside the bed. The full cup of coffee sloshed over the table and ran in a stream to the floor.

The commotion brought two nurses running into the room—both stopping a foot inside the door with their mouths gaped open. Daisy was still giggling, and Sam was still trying to get on top of her.

One of the nurses quickly turned and shut the door before turning to her stupefied partner. "Miss Darcy, you get out there and make light of this while I clean up in here. Don't you say nothing now—I mean it."

"Yes, mam." The younger girl left out and shut the door behind her.

The large black lady turned around, hands on her hips, looked at the big-eyed couple and the smiling dog and burst out laughing. "Whoo, lawd, this bunch in here sure knows how to make a bored old lady's day." She giggled, then as serious as she could force on herself, she eyed the perp—"Now you," she glanced up at Mitch, "which is it, a miss or mister?"

"This is Samson," he replied, a bit embarrassed.

Back down at Sam— "Mister Samson, you best mind yourself while me and your man there clean up. Now if you didn't have breakfast yet, you can get over here and have it now. Otherwise, don't you budge til I say so."

It was all Mitch could do to keep from laughing out loud.

She pointed at the badge on her uniform. "See this, Mister Samson? It says, Stoney, D.O.N. That means Director of Nurses. Stoney here is the boss, so you best be minding me. Now you going to eat that?" She pointed to the floor.

Mitch let go of his collar and when he eyed the scattered food, she stooped over and picked up a piece of bacon. "Come on and get it. Nobody here is mad."

He cleaned the floor, coffee and all, within seconds, then obediently went to sit beside Mitch.

Neither Daisy nor Mitch had moved a muscle since Stoney entered the room, but Mitch didn't wait to be told again. He retrieved paper towels from the bathroom and got busy with the mess on the table and putting dishes back on the tray.

Stoney pressed the intercom and ordered a janitor— "not later—right now" —to disinfect the floor and table.

"Miss James, I was actually on my way in here to tell you one of my best jokes to try to get a smile on that face of yours. But I saw Samson there did it for me. He even made me laugh. And, you know, Miss James, that's a good day when I can laugh like that. You best be remembering that. Laughter is a healer for the soul." She patted Daisy's leg and proceeded to pull the tape off of her wrist.

"You've been released. I'll get this mess out of your hand and you can get dressed to go. The paperwork should be ready in a few minutes."

Before Daisy could react to the fact that she hadn't seen her clothes, Mitch raced to the wide window sill where he'd been standing, picked up the bag he'd carried in and set it on the bed beside her. "Clothes to wear home."

There it was again. He watched as she averted her eyes, face drawn like she felt sick. She attempted to look at him, but only nodded and put her attention on what Stoney was doing with the tubes in her hand. It dawned on him then that not one word had been spoken between them since he and Sam had come in the door. There hadn't been much chance, but still—something was way out of kilter with her. *What? What was wrong?*

He wasn't about to upset her over this issue. She'd been through more than enough. He was just so thankful to Laura Brandon for her insight in suggesting he buy her a full set of new clothing—even giving him her probable sizes. Thankfully one of the salesgirls looked exactly her size in every way and she selected everything she'd need from head to toe to walk out of this place and get home with her dignity intact. That's all he cared about—making sure she felt comfortable.

"Okay...come on, Sam." He looked at the side of Daisy's face. "I'll take him for a walk and bring the car up to the front door." He paused, still looking at her, but she didn't respond other than to nod her head. "I'll be back in a few minutes," he said as he and Sam went out the door.

Supposing it would be an hour or so before she was ready to go—Mitch and Sam sat for a while in the car just outside the front entrance of the hospital. The pain inside him was trying to turn to anger. He knew if Daisy's attitude toward him didn't change, he was going to have to make a hard choice. He couldn't force himself on her—He *wouldn't—ever.* For the first time, he let himself think that Daisy might not truly feel the same about him.

She was lonely. Vulnerable. She had no family. Her reaction to him back at the ranch was possibly just a yearning for someone to show her kindness—acceptance.

He sat up straight when he saw a nurse push her out in a wheelchair. At the sight of her, all doubt about her feelings toward him drained out. She was wearing the clothes he'd found her in and the blue bag with the ones he'd bought her was setting in her lap.

Slowly he opened his driver door and got out. He opened the passenger door and stood back while the nurse helped her into the front passenger seat and closed the door.

"Thank you, mam. He nodded toward the attendant and went around and got in.

Sam had stayed quiet, stretched out on the back seat.

There was silence for a few seconds. Then he cut his eyes toward her. "I see you found your clothes."

"They washed them and sent them to my room with my dismissal papers." She held up the blue bag. "I don't need these."

"Okay." He felt like wadding it up and tossing it out the window. Instead, he took the bag and gently slid it up on the dash of the car. "You'll have to tell me which way to point these wheels."

"I'd like to go by the Sheriff's Department and leave my mother's keys with them. I have no need for them."

He punched in the information on his cell for directions and headed that way. He took the keys inside for her and learned that Arlene had been transferred from the jail to a mental health hospital about three hundred miles away.

"Thank you for everything, Mitch. I truly appreciate everything you've done." She glanced over at him. "Did you drive all this way?"

"No. I flew and rented a car—but I returned it yesterday."

"Maybe you should drive to a rental agency and get another or go to the airport now. Sam and I can drive on to my house."

He started the engine and headed out of the parking lot without even glancing her way. "Not today, young lady. I'll get you and Sam boy home, then I'll get back to mine." It came out a little more terse than he liked.

They lapsed back into silence.

Mitch was done with this girl's treatment of him. She would have to come to terms with what her life had been before she could move forward and be happy. But she apparently was not interested in his help—or in him, period.

Within a couple of hours, Mitch parked Daisy's Civic in her driveway and got out to walk Sam while she unlocked her door and went inside.

Daisy kept her focus on everything except the man walking her dog. She hoped he wouldn't come inside. She turned on lamps and pushed the air conditioner down to cooler—hurrying to get everything in order so he wouldn't think he needed to help her.

Looking out the open front door, she watched him finish a phone call and shove his cell into his jeans pocket. After he rubbed and patted all over Samson, he brought him to the door and handed his leash to her.

"I have a ride coming to take me to the airport. You take care of yourself, Daisy. You have my number if you need me." He turned and walked down the drive and a short way down the road until he was out of her sight.

Daisy slowly closed the solid wood door and for the first time since getting out of that closet, she allowed her thoughts and emotions to surface. Never would her life be whole again. Never would she love again. She turned and leaned her back against the door, feeling the weight of an empty life. On trembling legs, she slid down the door until she sat on the floor and cried gut wrenching sobs. *Mitch. Oh Jesus—Mitch.* He was gone forever, and she couldn't fix it.

Mitch drove his dually through the dude ranch gate just after midnight. His trip home had been uneventful—but long and depressing. There were so many questions rolling around in his head that didn't seem to own an answer.

He went straight to the bunkhouse. Clint's vehicle was gone, and he was thankful for the solitude tonight.

Entering the cabin, he knew Clint and Abby had already moved out. The interior was cold and dark—matching his insides perfectly. He wanted to move through the darkness and fall into bed—no thoughts, just sleep.

But first, he had to touch base with his Greatest Friend. He sat down at the small table with only a stream of moonlight coming through the tiny slit in the curtains.

"Lord Jesus," he began, then couldn't think of anything to say. After several minutes, he just got real honest—"You know how I'm feeling. I don't feel like praying. But I praise You anyway because You said to. And, I thank You, too, but You know I don't feel real thankful."

Tears suddenly filled his eyes and spilled over as a deep sob tightened his chest. He tried to swallow it away, but more came.

He didn't know how long he sat there after his tears ran out, but he was surprised at the easiness that had settled in his body—a peace that can only come from God's presence.

"Would You tell me what to do now, Lord? I love her. You know that. I just don't know how to go on."

Suddenly there was that image again of Daisy curled up unconscious in the floor of that closet. He could actually see himself standing there looking down at her. "Why do I keep seeing her like that, Lord? Is this the only reason she came into my life—to be her rescuer from that place?"

He got up then and went to bed—and was asleep almost before his head hit the pillow.

The next morning before sunup, he was in the barn at the Double OO feeding Tuff and preparing for a full work day. He heard someone shuffling around by the tack room, then pushing a squeaky wheelbarrow his way. He looked up and spotted Les Kane craning his neck around the corner.

"Hey, Mitch…didn't know you were back, but sure am glad you are. You working for me today or Jesse?"

"I figure some of both. Looks like Clint and Abby are gone."

He nodded, "Them and two of my hands left yesterday."

Mitch raised his eyebrows. "No kidding?"

"Well, Clint's dad had a heart attack, so they hurried and loaded up and left yesterday. Mike and Todd had a family tragedy in Oregon. Being brothers—it took them both. Mike said they most likely wouldn't come back this way. They didn't last two full weeks. Not sure either of them were cut out for this life anyway."

"Well…you know I'll fill in every way I can."

"Thank you, Mitch. Appreciate you. Jesse told me and Judd what happened with Miss James. Tough deal."

"It could have ended worse. She's physically all right. Might take time otherwise."

Mitch was saddled and began leading Tuff outside to mount. "Where are the boys going to be?"

"Head toward the back ninety—you'll see them. I'll catch up with you soon as I feed this barn."

He nodded and trotted out toward Les's foreman's log cabin. He really liked Les. He and his wife, Kaitlyn, were both as down to earth as they come. It wouldn't surprise him to see her and Judd's wife, Toni, out on the range today helping out. Those women were excellent riders and had no qualms about getting dirt under their fingernails. Daisy would be just like them in that respect.

But he didn't need to be thinking about her today. *Keep your mind on your business, boy. Eyes on the Lord. That's all you need to do.*

It felt good to be in the saddle, on Tuff, riding into the almost sunrise. He would be fine today. His goal was to work so hard until bedtime, he couldn't stay awake to miss—her.

As he passed the foreman's house, he noticed there wasn't so much as a porch light on. If he didn't know the log home was there, he would never have seen it at all. But he couldn't remember *ever* not seeing lights on—if it was just out of the corner of his eye.

Something was arresting his attention to the point he reined Tuff to a stop and squinted his eyes into the darkness surrounding the house. He was a good two hundred yards away along the edge of the large stock pond. Slowly he walked his horse toward the house. The front door was wide open. There was no light—no sound. He dismounted. Dropping Tuff's reins in a ground tie, he walked towards the porch, stopping one move short of the bottom step.

In that moment, all hell broke loose. A shadowed figure, slightly shorter than Mitch, jumped over the three steps and let out a surprised yelp when it busted face first into Mitch.

Mitch took one step backward before stiffening his body against the onslaught—He took advantage of the man's shock—grabbed his shoulders and body-slammed him to the ground. He figured he could apologize later after this person proved he was supposed to be running out of the foreman's quarters in the pitch darkness.

But that idea vanished when the intruder began scrambling to get on his feet and run at the same time.

Mitch sent him to the ground again, then jerked the whimpering weasel back up where he got a look at his face in the breaking daylight.

"Mike Sims. What are you doing here?"

He caught movement to the left side of the house and saw another person running and disappear into the woods. Mike broke loose from his grasp and ran, but Mitch let him go when Kaitlyn Kane hit his mind. He ran up and stopped inside the open door.

"Kaitlyn?"

He flipped the light switch beside the door. Apparently, the power had been shut off. He ran back out and around the side of the house to the box on the pole. The usual outside lights and menagerie of lamps inside came on when he pushed the lever. Running back around to the front, Les was jumping off his horse, confusion etched in every crease of his face.

"Find your wife, Les. Intruders had shut off the lights and broke in here. One of them was Mike Sims. I saw him."

Before he stopped talking, Les had run up the steps and disappeared inside.

Mitch went out and grabbed his radio out of his saddlebag and informed A.J., who was already on the back ninety, where to go and try to intercept the culprits.

"Judd are you copying this?" He figured the boss had his radio on.

"Yes. I'm phoning the Sheriff's office now. Do we need an ambulance?"

"Don't know yet."

"I'll get one dispatched. Be right there."

Mitch stuck his radio in his back pocket and went inside.

"Kaitlyn." Les's spurs jangled heavily as he ran down the hallway. "Kaitlyn!"

It was quiet for a couple seconds after Les pushed open the bathroom door and disappeared inside. "Baby? Baby?" Les's voice was softer and soothing.

Mitch knew she was in there and stood still just outside the door, praying this wasn't going to turn out bad.

Les went to his knees beside his wife while she sat on the floor just outside the shower. Her hair was dripping wet and the top coverlet off their king bed was draped around her. She wasn't crying—just shocked with wide eyes staring into her husband's.

"I'm not hurt. I'll be alright," she said, unemotionally and strong.

"Let's get you up." He lifted her to her feet, keeping the coverlet fully around her. Leading her out and toward the bedroom, he saw for the first time the mess strewn across the floor from cabinet and desk drawers being emptied. He wondered how that bed cover ended up around her in the bathroom.

She stopped for several seconds when she saw Mitch and glanced at him before quickly looking the other way. Les led her into the bedroom which was ransacked as well. He gathered up her clothes and she dressed without either saying a word.

Mitch had gone back outside where Judd and Toni were driving up. The front door was still open, and the strewn mess could be seen inside.

"What in sam hill happened?" Judd asked.

At that moment, Les and Kaitlyn came out the front door. "I'm all right. I'm not hurt," she announced, but kept her eyes averted from everyone.

Mitch had seen that exact same look on Daisy's face the past couple of days. She'd kept her eyes averted from him just like Kaitlyn was doing now. Was it shock? Was it a reaction to fear?

Two sheriff department vehicles followed by EMS came around the corner. They were being led by a pickup driven by one of the barn hands. Judd had sent him to the road to watch for them.

Les hadn't tried to question Kaitlyn, knowing she would have to give an account to the Sheriff again.

The radio on Judd's belt squealed as the voice of AJ came on. "We've got a couple of yahoos—Sims brothers no less—hog tied and squalling like we might have threatened to brand em. We're located a good country block from the old jeep trail by the north gate. Caught em before they got back to their vehicle at the gate."

"Sit on em, AJ. I'll bring the sheriff around there."

"10-4."

"Everybody heard that?" Judd spoke to the group gathered around him.

Heads nodded.

The sheriff turned to his two deputies, "Go get those boys. Book em in and I'll finish up here."

Judd nodded and went to his dually to lead the patrol car around. He wanted a chance to see those hoodlum brothers before they were taken away.

\*\*\*

# CHAPTER TEN

The sheriff stepped over to Kaitlyn. "Mrs. Kane, I'm Glynn Davies. I know you've had a terrible scare this morning. Were you hurt in any way? I have EMS here…"

"No. No…I'm fine. I wasn't hurt. Thank you." She glanced at him then settled her gaze at the ground.

"All right. I need to know what you can tell me about what happened here. Would you like to sit down or talk more privately?"

"No, I'm fine right here. I was in the shower and the lights suddenly went out. I stepped out to go find my flashlight and someone was standing in the doorway. He shined a flashlight on me, and I sat down on the floor…I tried to…cover myself. I heard a lot of noise in the other part of the house, but he kept shining his light on me and just staring at me."

Mitch noticed that not once did she look up at the sheriff while she was talking—or anyone else for that matter. She stared at the ground.

"He…told me to stay quiet and not to move. He left but came back and dropped a cover over me. He said he was sorry. Then he left and closed the bathroom door. I heard so much noise and voices, but I couldn't understand what was said." She paused for several seconds. "The next thing I remember is Les kneeling down in front of me. That's all I know."

She continued to look at the ground in front of her, but eagerly accepted her husband's arm around her.

"Okay, thank you, Mrs. Kane. That'll be all. I promise you— justice will be served quickly. I'm very sorry this happened to you."

He directed his words to Les— "One of our investigators will be here shortly. He'll need access inside and he'll get a statement from you and from this gentleman." He glanced at Mitch.

"Mitch Corry, sheriff." Mitch stepped toward him to shake hands.

"Glyn Davies."

"I'll be around here—tell what I KNOW…"

That last word burst out of his mouth as a sudden force slammed into his back. He wheeled around as all sixty pounds of SaraLou hit his front side with equal force and happy dog cries. Mitch couldn't keep the broad grin off of his face as he patted her face and ruffled her fur around her neck and shoulders.

He glanced around, expecting to see Clint or Abby, but it seemed she was alone.

"Where'd you come from, young lady?"

"Beautiful dog," the sheriff said to Mitch as he headed for his patrol car.

SaraLou was overjoyed at seeing Mitch and continued jumping on him and crying.

"Okay, pretty girl settle down. Sit."

She knew that word and promptly sat beside him, but never took her wide eyes of devotion off of his face. He wondered then where her puppies were.

Toni Luke had sat on the steps, in case she was needed while Judd was gone with the deputies. She went to SaraLou and kneeled down beside her. "I'm glad you're back, Mitch. This girl has been depressed—constantly looking for you." She ruffled her fur. "But she's sure happy now."

Toni stood. "Don't worry about your puppies. They've all been staying at our house while you were gone."

Mitch turned his head from side to side looking for whoever Toni was talking to.

"Jenny's been having a blast with all those furry babies. I'll give you a heads up—if you haven't promised them all yet, Jenny wants one and Abby does, too, for little David. They're so darn cute!"

"Fine with me, but Clint is who you need to talk to."

Toni leaned toward Mitch and in low tones said, "SaraLou refused to load up with Clint when they left. He said she had a thing for you and by all indications just now—he was right. He said to tell you that you don't have to wait for his will to be probated and I'm guessing you know what he's talking about."

He swallowed at the lump in his throat as he looked down into those pleading, marble-blues, realizing for the first time just how attached he had become to this furry little girl. Somehow, she made his world light and bearable.

Within another hour, all was done, and Mitch took his side-kick back to her puppies at Judd and Toni's home, promising her he'd be back before dark for her and her brood.

The evening was cool, the promise of a north front coming in. Mitch propped his booted feet up on the log railing and leaned back in the squeaky antiquated rocker. The sun was gone— replaced with a thin haze that blocked out the fullness of moonlight. He stared at the tall pines surrounding this little bunkhouse—the darkness around him only interrupted by the dim yellow porch light—and wondered if Daisy would feel safe in a place like this.

He knew she loved his cowboy lifestyle and had expressed to him more than once that she hated the thought of going back home. She was a natural on horseback, wishing she could ride every day for the rest of her life. She had told him that. And what he had seen in her eyes that night—her soul had met and melded with his in one moment. He had felt it. She felt it.

But she'd left without a word to him—went back home where she didn't want to go. She went to visit a woman who she already knew despised her and wanted to hurt her—maybe kill her. And nearly did.

He also knew above all; Almighty God had directly led him to where she was imprisoned. The timing was impeccable and the journey of getting from this ranch to Texas and into a house, then to the closet where she lay dying. *Why God? Maybe I shouldn't ask You why—but, I want to know.*

For the first time in his life, he felt broken inside. His life had been simple, surrounded by nature—cows, horses, dogs—the best people on earth. *Broken* shouldn't be an adjective he could use on himself without feeling shame for thinking it.

Daisy was another thing. She had every right to feel broken—feel like she'd been cheated out of her childhood. He could only imagine what her young life had been like raised by a vile, mentally deranged mother. She was fractured in different ways.

"Lord, why is she rejecting my help?" He closed his eyes and focused all his senses on his Father. He was desperate for an answer and sought the One who had it.

Again, the same image of Daisy laying on the floor of that closet—of him standing there for the first seconds of opening the door, formed in the front of his mind. Then, another image followed that one—Kaitlyn's face staring hard at the ground in front of her house this morning.

His eyes popped open, breaking the images of his inner sight—but the revelation that popped into his mind startled him. He straightened in the rocker, sitting up on the edge of the chair as if he would jump up and take off somewhere.

When SaraLou pushed on the rickety screen door and appeared, on alert, in front of him, he wondered if his sudden move was also voiced aloud. She whined, staring up at him with her eyes furrowed in concern.

"It's all right, girl. Nothing's wrong out here." He rubbed her face and head and she curled up between his boots. "Exhausted, aren't you?"

Letting her rest up from *mama duty,* he sat still awhile longer, but pondered the insight he'd just received—believing God had given him the answer.

When he'd first opened the closet door and saw Daisy curled up and unconscious on the floor—there was an obvious urine odor where she'd been forced to wet her clothes. Not once had he thought of it again—only in that one second.

It hit him like a sharp squeeze in his heart. She was embarrassed. She was ashamed, knowing he had found her in that condition. And Kaitlyn had the same look of shame on her face this morning.

*Oh, Jesus—forgive me. I should have realized this.*

Restlessness took him over. He had to go to Texas. He understood now and he could fix this. He thought about driving into range of a tower where he could call her, but knew he needed to deal with this face to face.

He sighed heavily. These two ranches were desperately needing him right now. Shorthanded was putting it mildly.

His boots straddled his sleeping compadre as he stood up. He stepped away from her just far enough to sink down onto his knees on the rough wood porch floor. *"Lord, I want to thank You for showing me what the problem is with Daisy. I'm kind of caught in a hard place here—so—I'm asking if You will make a way for me to clear this up with her.  And, while I'm down here, I pray for Arlene James and also those Sims brothers—that You would bring them all to salvation in time. I pray in Jesus's Name. Thank You. Amen."*

He got to his feet, nearly tripping over SaraLou. She had moved to sit behind him as though to say *I've got your back.* "You're a good girl. Come on, let's turn in. God's going to figure this out for us."

Jesse Brandon quietly shucked his boots at the kitchen door, hung up his hat and coat and headed straight for the shower. It was close to midnight when he crawled into bed. He groaned as he lay flat on his back and concentrated to get his muscles relaxed.

Laura shifted her position and turned on her side toward him. "I wish I could make it easier on you out there, Jess."

"Unless you got two or three more of you hiding in the closet—don't see where you could do more. Jesse Jr and Anna are filling in some huge gaps for us outside of their regular chores."

He rolled over to face his wife and they looked into each other's eyes for a long time. He brushed his large, calloused hand across her cheek and hated how the intensity of love he had for this woman could feel painful at times. He truly wouldn't want to be alive on this earth without her.

"The work load should get lighter now," she added. "School's back in and the guests are about to end for the season. God's been so good to us here."

"That's a fact, Ms. Laura. Extra Good. I just hope things settle down for a while. This has been a crazy summer."

She smiled at his face in the darkness. "I've seriously thought about writing a book about our adventures over the years. Maybe we could star in our own movie about us."

His groan was deeper and louder this time. "Spare me, woman. Once around for some of this stuff is plenty. Don't make me relive it."

"Well, you could be a stand-in for the love scenes with me, couldn't you?"

He snorted. "Only if you don't want your otherwise leading man to get the snot beat clear out of him."

She chuckled. "I'll take that as a yes. Oh…and we have a single guest coming in next week for a few days. I guess this will be the last reservation for the season."

"That's nice. How many is that for the grand finale?"

"Three cabins and one teepee."

"Yeah. Ok." He was quiet long enough that she thought he was asleep.

"Who did you have in mind for the *otherwise* leading man?"

A grin split her face until it almost became audible. "Well, honestly I would love me some Clark Gable."

He didn't say anything.

"You know, *Gone with the Wind.*"

"Yeah, I know. You'll need a shovel to get him for the role." He paused. "But really, *who?*"

"Are you laying there working up a jealousy over me and my leading man from a novel I haven't written yet?" She burst out laughing. "I appreciate your confidence in me, but do you know how really old I'll be before I could get my first sentence written—

And then I can probably hawk it to *Clark* myself for a movie deal."
She rolled onto her back and laughed like she hadn't done in a
while.

He raised up and put his face over hers. "Honey, I think this
conversation fell off into the canyon a while back."

She laughed harder, covering her eyes with one hand. "Maybe
your half did. I'm grave yard serious, ma…myself."

He put his mouth next to her ear and so seriously whispered
while she shook with hysterical laughter—"Honey, you and I are
the old wise ones of the family. If *we* lose our minds, the
*ranch…will…fold.*"

That did it. Tears streamed down the sides of her face onto her
hair and pillow. "Oh geez, Jesse, I think it's too late," she
squealed, about to lose her breath.

He rolled her away from him onto her side and with both arms,
he pulled her tightly into them.

Just when she was about to get control of herself, she felt his
body shaking and heard him giggle behind her head. It was all
over.

Soon they both laughed themselves to sleep.

The sun was casting a dim light across the eastern horizon when
Laura opened her eyes the next morning. Jesse was already gone,
and the house was too quiet, telling her that everyone had left
before dawn to start chores—except her. She had been joining the
ranch work force with the rest of her family for most of the
summer due to High Point and their neighboring Double OO being
shorthanded for one reason or another.

She headed into the kitchen to grab a fast cup of coffee, only to
find a note stuffed inside her favorite cup— *Enjoy your Saturday
morning. Me and the kids have got this. See you at lunch. Jess*

Laura smoothed her fingers across the words on the paper—her
cowboy's familiar handwriting that made her feel guilty because of
the amount of work she knew was outside—and made her feel
loved beyond reason by a man who deserved so much more than it
seemed she was able to provide. Jesse was her gentle giant, a

humble soul that was her one and only forever mate. Not in this lifetime would another walk in his shoes with her. That's why his little show of jealousy made her laugh so hard last night. She doubted that he had a clue how bad she had it for him.

Sliding the note into her pajama pocket, she carried a cup of coffee into her sitting area and accepted her family's gift of a day off.

Her mind drifted to the phone call she'd received from Daisy James yesterday. She hoped she had done the right thing by encouraging her to come back up for a few days. Daisy had serious issues that she needed to work through—and after hearing about her ordeal with her mother the past few days, maybe pushing her toward Mitch was not what *he* needed. Busy-bodying was not her cup of tea but urging Daisy to come now for the last week of the season and clear the air with Mitch just seemed to fall out of her mouth. She had heard Mitch's story of what took place in Texas when he called her from there and it seemed apparent that God had a Hand in him being in the right place at the right time to save her.

She had prayed yesterday after Daisy's call and asked God to take control of all this and forgive her if she'd overstepped her bounds. So—she needed to leave it all in His capable Hands and stop the worrisome thoughts. Mitch Corry and Daisy James were adults and God was God. Enough out of her!

Sipping her steaming coffee, she mentally planned out her and Granny Martha's next couple of days getting the cabins and teepees cleaned and ready for the last group of dudes—and thanked her Lord for Hank and Martha Walton!

Mitch was used to hard work. But he didn't think he'd ever worked so fast for so many hours as he had the past several days. After finishing an early morning trail ride into the canyons with a string of about ten—most of them, first time riders—then, untacking and caring for the horses afterward—he would head to the Double OO and pull a few hours riding for their brand.

It was well after dark before he dragged his body into the bunkhouse, fed SaraLou, showered and fell into bed. It would all start again long before the sun came up. He mentally ran down the list again, hoping for a way to make a quick trip to Texas:

Beau Vance's wife, Carly, had a family emergency in her home state of California—taking him off of the work schedule indefinitely. Beau was the best roper in the state, inheriting his ability from his champion rodeo roper dad, Webber Vance.

And now, the two Sims boys who had hired on for the Double OO just a couple weeks ago were both behind bars. Neither one could cowboy worth their paychecks and obviously never meant to work—but to case out the place.

And of course—Clint and Abby's life had to move on.

The ranch was bare bones for working cowboys, concluding that he'd better get some sleep.

It had been two weeks since Mitch's rescue mission in Texas. He hadn't heard a word from Daisy and thankfully had been too busy and exhausted to think about her—*not more than a few times a day, anyway.*

After attending cowboy church services earlier that Sunday morning, he was told to rest up a couple days and be back on schedule Tuesday morning—but to stay on call til then. That suited him fine. He'd well earned a few hours of butt-time.

He'd opted to fix a ham sandwich out of his own fridge for Sunday lunch. Hank and Martha were dishing up leftovers from the past week for whoever wanted it. There were no dudes to cook fresh for until Tuesday. After this next week, the *dude* part of the ranch would be shut down for the season.

The better part of the afternoon was spent making up to SaraLou for his being away so much. Her puppies were beginning to crawl around and taste the soft meaty dog chow he left out. Mama was already trying to wean them from lunching with her around the clock. She was tired, too.

Beau and his family were due back tomorrow. That was the best news he'd had in a while.

He carried a fresh smoking mug of coffee out to the porch and moaned when he lowered his body into the rocker. He laughed and shook his head at how much he was reminding himself of his dad.

The late evening was beautiful with the first few stars flipping on their night lights. With boots propped on the porch railing, one foot crossed over the other, he was too comfortable 0to bother getting up at the sound of the truck approaching the side of the cabin. It wasn't a loud, grinding dually. Sounded more like the old ranch pickup. The motor shut off and somebody opened the squeaky door to get out. He thought it strange how many little sounds you don't hear when you can see the action. He cut his eyes toward that side of the house, watching to see who was driving that old banger. It wasn't driven much these days.

He froze when he saw her step around the side of the cabin in full view of the front porch. Those bouncy blonde curls were pulled back in a loose ponytail. She looked—beautiful. It didn't escape his notice that she was wearing the denim calf-length jeans and pink short-sleeved shirt he had bought her to wear home from the hospital.

His coffee cup had paused a breath from his mouth. Once his shock at seeing Daisy suddenly appear in front of him subsided enough, he set the cup on the floor beside his chair and slowly took his feet off the rail. He couldn't take his eyes off of her face—could barely breathe.

She stopped when their eyes met, unsure of the look on his face—unsure that his expression said she was welcome. Maybe he didn't like her in these clothes after she was so ungrateful to him. Her heart raced as she watched him so slowly come down the porch steps and walk toward her. When she wanted to look away, his eyes held hers steady until they stood a couple of feet apart.

"Daisy." His voice was deep and low toned. "Are you really standing here?" He swallowed hard as his expression changed from disbelief to a soft awe.

"Hello, Mitch."

"I had no idea you were coming."

"I know. I…I was afraid you might not want to see me, and I needed to tell you how…" She paused several long seconds. "Mitch…I'm so sorry."

He wanted to grab her and wrap her up in his shaking arms, but held still, not sure she was meaning to come back to him.

"Daisy…you have nothing to …"

"Yes…I do. I treated you so mean, and you saved my life…you took care of me. I was so ashamed of…what you saw…what…" She lowered her eyes and was quiet.

She didn't finish, but he knew. Watching her rub her arms, he noticed the sun was gone and the air was chilly. He reached out and she put her small manicured fingers into his wide, warm palm. "Let's go in where it's warm."

Inside he moved her to sit on the table bench while he flipped on a couple of lamps and hurriedly put a match to the starter log in the fireplace.

Disappearing into the back room, he emerged with a couple of heavy quilts and tossed them on to the small couch, then pushed it closer in front of the fire. He knew he was taking a chance on her panicking and running out—but to his surprise, she got up and picked up a quilt and folded it into a long smooth pallet and laid it flat on the floor in front of the couch.

She turned to face him, looking him straight in the eyes. "We never did get to have our campout."

He felt his own smile go all the way to his toes. "Are you hungry? I've got ham and bread and…ham."

"No thanks. I grabbed a plate at the chuckwagon."

"Coffee? Hot chocolate?"

"Hmm…hot chocolate sounds awesome."

He took her arm and settled her onto the floor with the sofa perfect for a backrest, before heading for the kitchen.

Minutes later, boots and shoes tossed aside, they sipped chocolate and watched the fire flicker and pop.

"How long will you be here, Daise?"

"I'm not sure yet. I have five days paid for."

"When do you go back to work?"

149

She shook her head. "I resigned my job."

He bent his leg and shifted around to face her, resting his elbow on the sofa. He rubbed her cheek with the back of his fingers, then grasped a lock of hair that had pulled out of her ponytail and pushed it behind her ear.

A tear escaped and dripped onto her cheek at the gentle touch of this man who possessed her heart and soul. There was so much against her—a past that she may never fully be free of—and she loved him too much to see him thrust into her nightmares and phobias—And the ugly way he had seen her that she knew he would never be able to unsee. She felt panic rising suddenly and realized she'd made a mistake coming here.

But he saw her face change and before she could move to get away, he caught her upper arms and held her still.

"No, Daisy. Not this time. Do you think I can't love you—be good to you?" He turned her body around to face him. "I want you to look at me."

She raised her head and looked into his eyes with pools of tears about to fall. He ripped the snaps open on the cuff of his shirt sleeve and held his arm up to dab at the fresh spill on her cheeks.

He softly laid his hands on her forearms bringing her gaze back up to his. "First off, yes, I opened that closet door and saw you laying in a ball and in a puddle of pee—dying, Daisy. I dragged your body out of that stinking death trap and could think of nothing except begging Almighty God not to take you to Heaven. I selfishly wanted you for myself—I wanted you to marry me and lay in my arms every night for a lifetime and make love to your beautiful body and soul for a lifetime. I've prayed that every day since—right up to today. You're feeling embarrassed at something that doesn't exist for me. Daisy—it never existed."

He paused a moment, but their gaze never broke from each other's. "How would you feel about me if you'd found *me* knocked out and in that same condition? What would you think about me now?"

Her eyes spread on him as she realized in that moment how childish she had been. Of course, she would not think bad of him. Maybe she'd love him all the more—if that were even possible.

"Daisy—I can't live my life without you. It would be meaningless. I want you here with me."

She gazed into the fire for a long minute before looking back at him. "Mitch— I need you to answer one question."

He nodded.

"What will you do when I wake up every night fighting or screaming in the throes of a nightmare—on our honeymoon—in a year or five years? How will you deal with that?"

His steady gaze remained fixed on hers for a long minute. "Can I show you my answer?"

The rugged warmth of his voice had a smile in it as though he had an easy answer. She nodded, not taking her eyes from his.

He reached an arm around her back and under her legs, lifting her effortlessly onto his lap. Wrapping her up in a steely hold with both arms around her—he pressed her body tightly into his and lay the side of his face on the top of her head. He rested his back against the couch and held her until he felt her fully relax, letting her weight press into him. When she began to cry, he continued to hold her tight without a word. Only sometime later when she was ready, he released his hold.

"You're safe, baby. You'll always be safe with me."

The firelight created a warm golden glow around the room, cocooning their bodies in an intimate safety net. Daisy had never felt so protected.

"Baby—you were raised to feel pointless—to feel like you had no value. That was all a lie that you were made to believe about yourself." His voice was gravelly but comforting—his words gently piercing into the buried secret places of her heart. "I need you to know that I get it—that I understand where you're at. You never got to be a child, a giggly little girl or teenager who was loved by her parents just because they were supposed to love you. You deserved that love, but that part of your life was stolen—by mental illness or the devil himself—And sadly you can never have those years back. I can't replace that. No one can." He paused a moment. "You don't need a parent now, Daise. But—I want to be your husband. And within our marriage, I want us to enjoy the laughter and silliness—savor life together. We'll grow through this side by side until you feel no more pain of loss."

He pulled her back and leaned forward so he could look into her face. A fresh swell of tears brimmed and spilled down her cheeks. His voice fell to a whisper. "That day will come, Daisy Mae. You *will* be free of nightmares and you *will* have the love you deserve for the rest of my life."

Time stopped at the words Mitch had just poured from his heart into hers. She knew he meant it—every syllable.

She slid an arm around his waist and splayed her open hand against the small of his back, pulling him to her in a tighter hug.

She heard him release a long slow breath and realized at that moment how much he needed her response—her touch—her love. And she had an overwhelming desire to give him all she had. But still, she couldn't stop the thought—*Would what she had to offer be enough? Could she love Mitch Corry the way he needed to be loved by a woman?*

Yes! She could—because she loved this man with all her heart, soul and body. And she knew he loved her.

When she tilted her head back to look into his face, a radiance lighted her features, creating a look he had never seen on her. Her smile said *yes*. Her eyes fired sparkles into his that said *yes*. And when his mouth claimed hers—she kissed him back with all the *yes* she possessed.

\*\*\*\*

# EPILOGUE

Two weeks later, amid shouts of well-wishes and showers of bird seed—Mitch and Daisy Corry loaded up and drove to the bunkhouse to change into warmer rough-out clothes and load up their camping gear. They headed for Judd Lukes's campsite and tent on the bluff overlooking the back ninety of the Double OO Ranch. Daisy had been as giddy as a kid in a toy store packing up for hers and Mitch's campout honeymoon.

Both ranches had come together, headed up by Jesse and Laura Brandon and Hank and Martha Walton, to shower the *orphan lovebirds,* as Granny Martha nicknamed them, with a simple and memorable wedding ceremony in the Cowboy Church.

Hank was moved to tears when Daisy shyly asked if he would walk her down the aisle and give her away. Andy Parker stood with his longtime friend as best man while Pastor Judd laughingly agreed to Mitch's request to *do the marryin'.*

A short reception was held on the pavilion with a Hank-made cake and lemonade before the couple loaded up and honked the truck horn all the way to the bunkhouse, where they would be living for the time being.

Within fifteen minutes, Mitch pulled up beside the tent and parked.

"Give me a few minutes." He jumped out knowing he'd have to do a little dusting-out in the tent before he could expect Daisy to be comfortable. He had opted for a night in Jackson Hole, but she wouldn't have it any other way. Pastor Judd had told him his hands were using the tent up until today so he dreaded what he would find in there.

Hurrying around to the front, he quickly unzipped the closed flap and drew the doorway wide open. He took a step back at first glance inside.

"Holy moly," he exclaimed.

"What's wrong?" Daisy walked up beside him and echoed— "Holy moly."

A sweet smell of fresh roses wafted out of the interior and a basket of snacks—wine and two wine goblets sat on the clean canvas floor of the tent in a bucket of melting ice.

They stepped inside to see a thick air mattress surrounded by red rose petals and made up with fresh, clean quilts and fluffy pillows.

"Well, God Bless those sneaky angels that did *this*," Mitch proclaimed.

He turned around and cupped his bride's face in his large, calloused hands.

She placed her hands over his and rubbed her cheek against the roughness of his palm. She wanted to laugh and cry at the same time with pure joy. "Tell me I'm not dreaming this," she whispered up at him.

He bent and kissed her upturned mouth, then licked his lips in grand exaggeration, smacking his lips loudly. "Can't say that. It *does* taste like a dream all right! And if you *are* dreaming, my beautiful lady, we're dreamin' together. So, just don't *ever, ever* wake up."

He let her go just long enough to turn around and zip up the tent door.